"You're safe, Darcie," Noah said.

Was she? Would this creep think she could identify him and come looking for her? Come after her with his gun, or even worse, try to strangle her again?

A full-on shudder claimed Darcie's body, and despite her efforts to fight back her tears, they started flowing. She tried to stop them, willed them away, but to no avail.

"Aw, no. Don't cry." Noah's arms went around her, and he drew her close.

She needed him. Just now. Not later. Never again. Just now.

He cradled her head and held her. She allowed herself a few more moments to take in the warmth and ease the chill from her heart, but when her tears fully subsided, she couldn't find an excuse to stay in his arms, so she eased free and looked up at him.

"Better?" he asked, his gaze tender as he pressed a wayward strand of hair behind her ear.

She didn't know how to reply, and silence hung heavy in the air. She didn't want to admit that outside his arms she felt afraid.

If she did, he would feel a need to protect her, and that wouldn't be good for either of them.

Susan Sleeman is a bestselling author of inspirational and clean-read romantic suspense books and mysteries. She received an RT Reviewers' Choice Best Book Award for *Thread of Suspicion*; *No Way Out* and *The Christmas Witness* were finalists for the Daphne du Maurier Award for Excellence. She's had the pleasure of living in nine states and currently lives in Oregon. To learn more about Susan, visit her website at susansleeman.com.

Books by Susan Sleeman

Love Inspired Suspense

First Responders

Silent Night Standoff
Explosive Alliance
High-Caliber Holiday
Emergency Response

The Justice Agency

Double Exposure
Dead Wrong
No Way Out
Thread of Suspicion
Dark Tide

High-Stakes Inheritance
Behind the Badge
The Christmas Witness
Holiday Defenders
"Special Ops Christmas"

Visit the Author Profile page at Harlequin.com for more titles.

EMERGENCY RESPONSE

SUSAN SLEEMAN

HARLEQUIN® LOVE INSPIRED® SUSPENSE

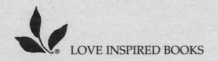

LOVE INSPIRED BOOKS

ISBN-13: 978-0-373-67750-4

Emergency Response

Copyright © 2016 by Susan Sleeman

www.Harlequin.com

Printed in U.S.A.

May the God of hope fill you with all joy and peace
as you trust in Him, so that you may overflow with hope
by the power of the Holy Spirit.
—*Romans* 15:13

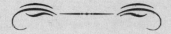

For my wonderful daughters, Erin and Emma.
As I wrote this book about parental loss, I was constantly
reminded of what amazing daughters you are and that
I am so blessed that God has put you both in my life.

ONE

Can't breathe. Must breathe.

"No." Darcie Stevens clawed at the beefy arm circling her neck like a hangman's noose, her fingernails raking over her attacker's fleshy arm.

Scratching. Ripping. Drawing blood.

It didn't deter him. He tightened his grip, cutting off the last of her breath. "Give it up. You won't win."

She worked harder to release the pressure on her windpipe. Struggled for oxygen. Any. Even the tiniest sip of cold February air. Found none.

Her vision blurred and she blinked hard.

No! Please, no!

Was this the end? Desperation set in. She had to try harder.

She elbowed his gut. One hard, firm jab to the midsection, her elbow sinking into his stomach.

He didn't move except to constrict his arm and draw her back more tightly against his flabby body. She felt a gun tucked into his belt pressing against her back.

No. No. No.

Did he plan to shoot her if he failed to choke her? She had to get away before he drew the weapon. But how?

Her shoes. Yes, her boots had spiky heels. They could do some serious damage. She stomped on his foot, grinding, pressing, digging for concrete.

"Uhhh," he grunted. His arm relaxed a fraction.

Yes!

She pressed her hands together like a diver and shot them up under his arm, pushing with all of her strength. Widening the gap.

One final push. She gave it her all and broke free. She gulped air and didn't waste time waiting to see what he might do, but took off down the sidewalk. Her steps, halting at first as she dragged in enough oxygen to pick up speed.

He followed her, the sound of his heavy footfalls reverberating in her ears. Her lungs were heaving with exertion. Her body begged to stop. To rest.

No. I can't let him catch me. If he does…

She wouldn't let that happen.

Please help me to go on.

Rain started to fall, pelting her face, soaking through her jacket. The moss-covered sidewalk threatened to take her feet out from under her. She focused on her shoes.

Careful now, one foot in front of the other.

She was making progress, but so was he. She could hear him coming closer. Closer. Step by step. Each footfall sounding like thunder in her ears.

The wind rushed past, carrying the echo of his heavy footsteps and masking his location. Could he have closed the distance? Was he readying himself to attack again? But why was he targeting her? What did he want? She didn't live in this part of town. He likely didn't even know her.

Was this attack random, like the woman who was mugged just down the street last week? A gang member had beaten her badly and she was still fighting for life. Was that this man's plan, too? Was he simply trying to subdue her then rob her?

Darcie couldn't let that happen. She churned her legs faster, harder. Her lungs screamed for relief. She couldn't think about that. She forced her concentration onto the rhythm of her feet.

Step. Step. Step.

Faster. Faster, she moved.

She risked a glance back. She had a small lead.

Thank You, God.

She took another quick look at her attacker, searching for details she could tell the police.

He was tall. Thick. Beefy. His skin was dark—Latino, she guessed. She returned her focus to her stride. She was running out of breath and slowing. He was panting hard, but he could still catch her.

Help me, God. Please. Help me.

The thudding footfalls suddenly stopped. Had he given up? Had she succeeded in tiring him out? Had God intervened?

Relief surged through her body, but she kept going. She had to. She wasn't safe yet.

A gunshot suddenly broke the quiet. A bullet slammed into the tree in the median. Wood fragments splintered and peppered her face. She closed her eyes for protection. Caught a toe in the cracked sidewalk. Plummeted to the concrete.

Oomph. She landed hard.

The rough surface ripped the skin from her palms and split the knees of her pants. She stayed on the ground, dazed for a moment, her brain a jumbled mess.

Another bullet bit into the concrete near her head. A jagged shard sliced into her neck. She cried out and protected her head with her hands. Her heart stuttered, feeling like it might stop, but she wouldn't give up. Couldn't give up. Couldn't just lay there knowing the next bullet would hit the mark.

But what could she do? She couldn't outrun a bullet.

Hide. She had to find a place to hide.

She pushed to her feet, started running again and searched the street. Run-down houses with peeling paint and weed-infested yards greeted her. No telling who lived in these houses, but she'd be safer inside. Or maybe someone would come out and help her if she pounded on a door.

Yeah, right. Not in this gang-infested neighborhood.

A bullet whizzed past her shoulder.

She glanced down the street. She could see her destination up ahead. Pilar's house. She was almost there. Could she make it before this creep shot her in the back?

Another bullet zipped past her shoulder.

She had to try. She kept going and hunched her shoulders to make herself a smaller target. Just a little ways to go and she'd reach Pilar's walkway where she could race inside to safety.

Shots kept flying.

Ping. Ping. Ping.

He was shooting like a madman, not even pausing to aim. She had to take cover. Now!

She dove behind a large utility box and curled into a ball. Sucking in air. Blowing it out.

Thoughts zinging through her mind as fast as the bullets flying overhead.

What could she do?

Think, Darcie, think.

Help. She needed help. Her teammates on the First Response Squad would know what to do. They were all trained law enforcement professionals, but not her. She was the team's paramedic and the only one without law enforcement credentials. Unfortunately, they couldn't get across town in time.

Noah. She could call Noah. He was already on his way to meet her at Pilar's house to talk to her about sweet little Isabel. As a homicide detective, he'd know what to do. He had to.

Darcie clawed through her purse until she grasped her phone. Her hands shook, blurring the screen, but she managed to press Noah's number.

"Lockhart," he answered.

"A man tried to strangle me," she managed to get out. "He's chasing after me now. He has a gun."

"Where are you?" Noah's voice was reassuringly cool and controlled.

"Behind a utility box close to Isabel's house."

The sound of her assailant's boots beating down the sidewalk drew her attention. She came to her knees. Peeked over the box. He was running toward her, his gun in his hand.

He spotted her. Paused. Lifted the gun. He fired. She ducked. The bullet flew overhead.

"Noah, he's shooting at me." She drew her legs up and wrapped her arms around them.

"I'm about a mile out," Noah said. "I'll be there as soon as I can, but you'll have to hold him off until I get there." The sound of Noah's siren coming to life filtered over the phone.

She wished she could hear it wailing down the street instead. "I—I—"

"You have a gun, Darcie. Use it."

"Shoot him?" Her? Fire a gun at someone? She was a paramedic—she treated gunshot wounds, she didn't cause them. Sure, she carried. She had to. Her FRS teammates insisted on it, and they'd taught her how to fire a gun, but they were always around so she never thought she'd actually have to use it. "I don't know if I can."

"Get it out, Darcie."

"I—"

"Do as I say, Darcie," Noah commanded. "No excuses. Put your hand in your purse and grab that gun. Now!"

His sharp voice broke her reluctance. She sat up, slid her trembling hand into the bag, finding the cool metal and curling her fingers around the grip.

"Got it." She lifted it out. Her heart kicked hard against the wall of her chest. The gun in her hand trembled.

Oh, God, please no.

"Noah, I can't shoot him," she whispered, her voice barely audible.

"Yes, you can. You have to. I—" His voice was cut off. She looked at her phone.

The call had disconnected. Most likely the signal had dropped—a common problem in this hilly neighborhood.

She was on her own again.

Her assailant's boots slapped the sidewalk.

Close now. Insistent. Threatening.

Thump...thump...thump.

He reached the box.

She dropped the phone. Lifted the gun. Held it out. The cold metal was foreign to her hands.

She raised it higher. Stretched out arms that felt limp, like a rubber hose.

"Oh, God, please," she begged, her heart in her throat. "Please don't make me shoot him."

Noah glanced at his phone. *Call dropped.* He'd lost Darcie. No surprise. He'd had problems with bad signals in this neighborhood before.

He slammed a fist into the wheel, his mind racing to find a way to help her. But maybe it was better this way. He could respond without having to split his concentration.

Right, better! How was it better not knowing if Darcie had managed to defend herself before some shooter took her out?

It wasn't. But he couldn't risk calling her back. Her ringing phone might give away her hiding spot, or distract her at the wrong moment.

He had to get to her, and fast.

He punched the gas. His sirens screamed and the light bar strobed in rhythm with his windshield wipers. Adrenaline coursed through his veins. His pulse beat triple time as anxiety climbed up his back and threatened to swamp him.

Eight years as a police officer and he'd never felt such fear. But then, a woman he cared about had never been under fire. He couldn't live with himself if anything happened to Darcie.

Father, please! Keep her safe. Let me arrive on time.

At the corner, he hung a hard right, the car hugging the curb and squealing. Onlookers watched from the sidewalk, but the road was clear of vehicles as a siren wailed from the south. Good, a patrol officer had responded to his radio call for backup and had arrived.

Noah rolled up on the scene moments later, taking in everything at once. The tired neighborhood. The shooter racing down the street, his weapon dangling from his hand. The lack of movement behind the utility box. The patrol officer bolting from his car in hot pursuit of the shooter.

Noah slid his vehicle in place next to the cruiser and forced himself to pause behind the door for safety as he thoroughly assessed the area. The air was heavy with tension as thick as the pounding rain. Dark and ominous skies hung overhead. A dog frantically barked in the background, the noise mixing with the wail of the sirens. The lone uniformed officer continued down the street, trailing the intruder, who was dressed in an oversize blue shirt and sagging jeans that looked like they might drop at any second. Noah made him as Latino, five-ten, two hundred and twenty-five pounds.

"Police. Stop," the officer shouted, then his voice came over Noah's radio as he reported to dispatch that he was on foot and needed backup.

Noah swung his gaze to additional patrol cars arriving from the other direction. The officers sprang from their cars and joined in the pursuit. The radio squawked with the first officer's voice, telling the others to set up a perimeter, and their lieutenant instructed them to switch radio channels to prevent other traffic from interfering with communications.

With several officers in pursuit of the suspect, Noah was free to check on Darcie, but he wanted to keep up on the action so he quickly adjusted his radio. Holding his weapon in defensive mode, his senses on high alert, he headed for the utility box.

By the time he crossed the road, his jacket was soaked and water dripped from his hair. He swiped the moisture from his face and cautiously approached. The last thing he wanted was for Darcie to mistake him for her assailant and fire at him. Or even let a nervous finger jerk the trigger.

"Darcie," he called out when he was still ten feet away. "It's me. Noah. The shooter is gone. You can lower your gun now."

She didn't respond.

Was he too late? Had she been shot?

Closing the distance, his heart slammed against his chest. "Darcie, are you okay? Did you lower your gun?"

"Yes." The barely audible word drifted over the box.

He nearly sagged with relief and stepped around the box. He found her slumped against the metal, her legs splayed out, her gun lying on her knees. Her chestnut hair hung wet and limp to her shoulders, and her usual smile was nowhere in sight. She stared ahead, her eyes vacant.

Her unfettered anguish stopped Noah cold. He'd had an awareness of Darcie for years, but neither of them was in a place for a relationship so he'd kept his interest to himself. But now, seeing her like this—emotionally ripped apart—it was all he could do not to wrap his arms around her and comfort her. The only thing stopping him was the certainty that she'd push him away.

"I'm going to take your gun now, Darcie," he said to keep from startling her. He gently took the weapon, but she didn't move. He clicked on the safety and shoved the gun into his belt. Still no reaction.

She was in shock. Not surprising after her ordeal.

He gently laid a hand on her arm to encourage her to look at him. "How are you doing?"

She didn't bat an eye. "I'm okay."

"No, you're not. You're in shock and need medical care."

She shifted to face him. "I'm the EMT here. I know what I need and I'll be fine." She fired him a testy look and started to rise.

Good. At least he'd gotten her to react, but he wasn't letting her get up.

"Hold on." He tightened his grip on her arm. "They're still chasing down the suspect. We'll wait here until he's apprehended."

Her eyes flew open, fear lurking in their depths. "Surely he won't come back here."

"With officers in pursuit, it's not likely, but you never know. He could double back. Could even try to barricade himself in one of these houses."

"Isabel," Darcie cried out and shook off his hand. "She could be in danger. I have to protect her. This guy, I think he's one of those gang members terrorizing the neighborhood. There might be others."

As much as Noah hated to admit it, Darcie's assessment was spot-on. In neighborhoods like this, gang members were like ants. Where there was one there were a bunch more. It meant Isabel and her grandmother, Pilar, were constantly in danger living here. In fact, he and Darcie had scheduled a meeting with Pilar today to discuss finding a safer place for the two of them to live. That would now have to wait until the immediate danger had passed.

Darcie started to rise. "I have to check on Isabel."

Noah rested a hand on her shoulder. "It's not a good idea to leave yet."

Darcie shrugged free. "Good idea or not, Isabel's in a wheelchair and I need to make sure she's protected."

His resolve wavered. Always did around Darcie. She had a heart the size of Texas—one of the things he admired about her—and she mothered everyone in her life. Though that had more to do with losing her child in a car accident a little over six years ago than anything. She would risk her own life in a heartbeat to make sure others were safe. He respected her for that, too. Along with her fierce personality that let no one get in her way. Like right now. If he didn't escort her to Isabel's house, Darcie would walk over there on her own.

He had no choice. She was staying under his protection until her attacker was apprehended. There was no question about that. None.

"Let me check things out first and then I'll take you to the house." He stood, keeping an eye on her for a moment to make sure she remained seated, and then made a careful survey of the area.

His radio squawked as one of the officers in pursuit reported his location about a mile north of their position and requested a lockdown of the nearby elementary school.

Now that Noah knew Darcie was okay, he wanted to get in on the action. He was a cop at heart. Had always wanted to be one, always would be one. And right now, he wanted to join his fellow officers in pursuit of a creep who'd terrified Darcie. To hunt him down, slap cuffs on him and toss him in the back of his car. Glare at him, too, and offer a few choice words for good measure. But at this moment, Darcie needed him more. Even if she wouldn't admit it.

He turned back to her and swallowed his emotions. "We're clear for now, but stay close to me. We'll go straight to the house and inside. Got it?"

A wooden nod was her only reply.

"Remember—" he paused for emphasis and offered his hand to help her up "—this situation is volatile and could change at any moment. Your life is still in danger and you need to follow my directions, not only for your safety but for Isabel's and Pilar's welfare, too."

Another stiff nod as she slid icy cold fingers into his hand. He tugged her to her feet and drew her close.

She winced and jerked free.

"You okay?" he asked, wondering if he'd hurt her, or if she just didn't want him to touch her.

She held up her palm. "I scraped my hands and knees when I fell."

Hot anger flared at the raw skin, but he swallowed it down as he'd done on the job countless times. "I know you can treat the abrasions yourself, but you could have other injuries that shock or adrenaline are masking. It's best to get you checked out by a medic."

She frowned. "Isabel and Pilar are far more important right now than spending time on a scrape."

She was right, but he'd still arrange for the medic. He urged her forward with an arm around her back. Her body trembled, sending his thoughts to the man dressed in blue. The thug who'd terrorized her. Her fear as she crouched in the rain waiting for him to kill her.

Noah's anger fired hotter. Once they found the shooter, Noah would make sure the creep paid for hurting her. "Did you recognize the man who attacked you?"

"No," she whispered. "But I can describe him."

"Great. If we aren't able to apprehend him today, we can get a sketch made."

She shot him a pained look. "Not apprehend him?"

"Hopefully that won't happen. Our officers are doing everything they can to catch him."

"I know."

"Do you have no idea why he attacked you?"

She shook her head hard, sending her ponytail softly whispering over his neck. "I figure it was just another random attack. You know. Like last week when that woman was mugged down the street."

When she was beaten within an inch of her life. He kept the last bit to himself so he didn't raise Darcie's apprehension. That and to stop his mind from wandering to the dire consequences if he hadn't been able to get a uniform here so quickly.

They started forward and he drew his weapon again for good measure. He pulled her closer. At five-nine—more like five-eleven today, in her heeled boots—she was only a few inches shorter than him. Her stride fell nicely into step with his and he caught a whiff of her fruity, tropical perfume. She'd worn the same scent since he'd first met her six years ago, when she'd joined the county's First Response Squad.

As a detective for the Portland Police Bureau, Noah didn't interact with the squad often, but he'd worked with them enough that he'd gotten to know everyone on the team.

Six members strong, they were all sworn deputies except Darcie. They performed regular law enforcement duties most of the time, but when they were needed in special crisis situations, they came together as a team. One specialized in bombs, another was a sniper, two of them were hostage negotiators and the last was the team leader. Darcie rounded out the team to provide medical support.

"Suspect's on the move. Going over the fence."

The officer's voice came over Noah's radio, startling Darcie.

Noah hugged her tighter and sped up. In a daze, she trudged alongside him. He felt like he was dragging her—maybe causing her pain. He hated the thought, but if that's what it took to get her safely inside, he'd do so.

They started up the walkway to the dilapidated bungalow Pilar rented from a slumlord who didn't care much about maintaining his property. Pilar kept it clean and tidy, but there was only so much she could do when the landlord never made necessary repairs. To make things worse, the cracking paint and crumbling cement walkways were decorated with graffiti and broken glass. Nearby neighborhoods were seeing rebirth, but the revitalization hadn't reached this street. The area was home to gang activities, which meant drugs and violence.

Darcie suddenly jerked back and pointed at the house. "Look. Bullet holes."

Noah spotted three punctures in the wall near the living room window. Likely stray bullets from the shooter's attack. His adrenaline fired higher. He moved Darcie behind his back and searched the area again.

The door suddenly swung open and he spun, gun pointed. Pilar's dark eyes, below scraped-back hair, widened and she took a step back.

Noah huffed out a relieved breath and hurried Darcie up the walkway. Pilar stood waiting, a towel wrapped around her arm. Blood seeped through the worn yellow fabric.

"Your arm." Darcie shot out from under his protection. "What happened?"

"A bullet…it came through the wall."

"Isabel?" Darcie's voice was deadly calm, but her eyes were wild with terror.

"She is fine. Hiding under her bed."

Darcie sighed out a breath and peered at Pilar. "Let me take a look at your arm."

Pilar lifted her hand and grimaced. "The bleeding has stopped."

"I still need—"

"Let's take this inside," Noah interrupted.

"But the sirens…the gunshots stopped after the police cars arrived. Aren't we safe now?" Pilar's hand shook as she supported her injured arm and backed inside. "What is going on? Is it another gang shooting?"

"I don't know the full details, but while the officers have everything under control, it's still safer to stay inside." Noah smiled again, putting on the officer persona he used to keep people calm in challenging situations. "Let's have Darcie check out your arm, and then we'll work on getting more details."

Pilar smiled, but it was forced. "You're both

wet and must be freezing. I'll get some towels before you catch your death."

"Seriously, Pilar? You've been shot," Darcie reprimanded. "You'll sit down and let me tend to the wound." Darcie gently prodded Pilar toward a worn armchair in the corner.

Noah took one last look outside, running his gaze up and down the road. Satisfied the women were safe for now, he closed and bolted the door. Double-checked it and glanced out the window for added measure. By the time he crossed the room, Darcie had settled Pilar in the chair. Darcie looked up at Noah, her focus clear once again. She'd shifted into rescuer mode, and with Pilar as a patient, Darcie could turn her focus outward. Maybe overcome her own shock.

"Can you check on Isabel?" she asked.

He really didn't want to leave the front of the house, but someone had to retrieve the little girl. He nodded, then headed for the bedroom and turned down the volume on his radio to keep from worrying the six-year-old.

Her room, the size of a walk-in closet, held a twin bed with a woven blanket and a painted nightstand topped with a multicolored lamp. The small wheelchair Darcie had secured for Isabel after Isabel had been injured on a callout sat empty by the bed.

He hadn't been at the incident but he'd heard a report that Isabel was living in deplorable conditions with her mother, Mayte. A social worker had come to the apartment to remove Isabel, but Mayte, high on drugs, had refused to hand over her daughter. A standoff occurred and the FRS responded. There was some concern about Isabel's health, so Darcie went in with Archer, one of their negotiators. His job had been to talk Mayte down, while Darcie's had been to make sure Isabel was okay. But Mayte clutched Isabel and backed onto an unsafe deck. The railing gave way and Mayte plunged two stories.

Darcie darted forward in time to catch hold of Isabel's calf and keep her from falling, but the wrenching motion injured Isabel's knee badly enough to require surgery. Mayte suffered a serious concussion. The good news was that the head injury kept her in the hospital long enough to go into drug withdrawal and to agree to rehab.

Now Isabel was once again in another traumatizing situation. The poor kid. She'd seen so much at her tender age. Way too much.

"Isabel, it's Noah," he announced to keep from scaring her even more as he stepped into the room. "It's safe to come out now. I'm going to help you into your chair."

He knelt by the bed and peeked underneath. Despite her living conditions or her recent accident, Isabel always had a big smile, and she flashed white teeth with a wide gap in the top.

"Hi, princess," Noah said.

"*Abuelita* put me here." Her smile faltered. "I was worried."

"Don't worry. Everything's okay." He reached under the bed and maneuvered her free, being careful not to bang her injured leg. He curled her into his arms and gave her a hug. She looked up at him, eyes wide.

"*Abuelita* got hurt."

"I know," he said, trying to play it down. "Darcie's taking good care of her."

"I thought maybe—" She shook her head and frowned. "You and Darcie weren't coming. Or you got hurt. Like that lady last week."

"No need to worry about that, princess. We're all just fine. And your grandmother will be fine, too." The vehemence in Noah's voice made her smile disappear. He didn't mean to sound so intense, but come on. No child should have their life invaded by man's brutality. "Let's go see Darcie, okay?"

"Yes, please." Isabel's face lit up and Noah's heart melted. There was something about this urchin that made him happy. If she survived all this trauma and still smiled, he should be able to do the same thing in his own life.

He settled her into the wheelchair and pushed her to the living room. Darcie ran her gaze over Isabel with a trained medical professional's eyes.

"Noah said you were here, but you really are," Isabel said, and smiled.

"Hold tight to the towel," Darcie ordered Pilar, then crossed over to Isabel.

Darcie squatted by the chair, and Noah saw her wince before she hid it. Her injuries bothered her more than she let on. She offered Isabel a beaming smile that utterly captivated Noah. In a situation that wasn't as dire as this one, he would...would what?

Do nothing. Exactly what he needed to do. What he'd done for years.

On the day he'd met Darcie, one look at her hit him like a battering ram, but he'd done nothing about it—would do nothing about it, other than swallowing down his feelings and acting professionally whenever he ran in to her.

Her smile widened even more and Noah had to step back to get a grip.

Concentrate, man. Concentrate. She's just a victim and this is just another callout. Do your job.

"Don't you know by now that nothing would

keep me away from seeing you?" Darcie asked Isabel.

She flung tiny arms around Darcie's neck. The child clung to Darcie as if she was her mother. With Mayte in rehab since her accident, Isabel had transferred her need for motherly love to Darcie. He wasn't surprised that Darcie hadn't been able to resist loving Isabel. Still, if Darcie realized how invested she'd become in Isabel's well-being, Darcie would shut down as she had since she lost her daughter. She avoided getting too close to anyone to avoid getting hurt.

Noah got that. He'd lost a son, too. Not to death, but to distance. He'd bailed on his pregnant girlfriend Ashley in college. Stupid move. But he was young and could barely get to class on time. How could he be responsible for a son?

He regretted it now. Every day. So he totally understood the wall Darcie put up to keep from caring and getting hurt again.

The hug ended and Darcie stood up.

"Can I talk to you for a minute?" he asked her and tipped his head at the far side of the room.

"Do you need me to call an ambulance for Pilar or have you already done so?" he asked when he couldn't be overheard.

"I have. They're on the way."

"Good. So will you be okay if I head outside to check on the action?"

A pained smile crossed her face, but she nodded anyway.

"Don't worry," he added. "I'll stay within view of the house. If you need me you can call out."

She gave just the barest hint of a nod as she grabbed his hand. Her still cold fingers squeezed weakly. "Thank you, Noah. For being here for us."

"It's what I do," he said and ignored how his heart warmed at her gratitude. "Lock the door behind me and stay away from the windows."

"You are leaving us?" Pilar cried out.

"It's okay," Darcie replied. "He'll be right outside and the danger has passed."

Noah nodded his agreement. Darcie's comment was technically true. The danger had passed. For now.

Only for now.

Darcie had gotten a good look at the creep who'd attacked her and could identify him. The man had to realize that as well. He had no qualms about attacking a woman, so if he evaded the officers today, he'd be more than happy to come after her again.

And the next time the creep got to her, Noah feared he'd succeed in silencing her for good.

TWO

Darcie couldn't quit shaking. Not from the chill in Pilar's hospital room, but from the memory of the attack. It would be a long time before she could forget about the crushing arm that had come around her neck. The bullets whizzing past. Even if she could forget, her neck throbbed and her knees and hands stung from the abrasions. Despite Noah's continued insistence that she needed medical attention, she'd tended to her own injuries while Pilar was in surgery for a repair to her shattered ulna.

Darcie tugged the collar on her shirt higher to hide the purpling marks from the attack. She would hate for the ugly bruises to scare Isabel or Pilar even more. Pilar was already staring at Darcie, her eyebrows in bushy arcs. She made the sign of the cross on her chest while mumbling something in Spanish. Darcie didn't speak Spanish, but she knew the sweet woman was praying for her.

That wasn't new. Pilar always offered up prayers for Darcie. It seemed odd that Pilar— a woman who had very little in life and had so many needs of her own to pray for—felt compelled to pray for her. It made Darcie uncomfortable to have someone treading on the edges of her personal life.

Needing a distraction for Pilar, Darcie spotted her iPad lying on the bedside table. Pilar worked from home and when her computer died a few weeks ago, Pilar had borrowed Darcie's iPad. As the EMTs wheeled her out of her home, she'd insisted on bringing the iPad with her, enabling her to work tonight.

Darcie tapped the screen. "Is the job still going well?"

The corner of Pilar's mouth tipped up. "Thanks to you. Your daily visits to Isabel have given me more time to focus on work. I am now making my quotas."

"Have you started getting paid yet?" Darcie hated to ask such a personal question, but she was skeptical about Pilar's new job. When Mayte went into rehab, Pilar had to leave her job as a cashier to care for Isabel, and this job seemed too good to be true. Darcie had been around the FRS team long enough to know that trusting people were often taken advantage of with work-from-home schemes.

Pilar's smile widened, wrinkling the crow's feet by her eyes. "My salary is directly deposited into my checking account as I finish each assignment."

"Good." Darcie had never been so thankful to be wrong. "It's great that you found the perfect job."

"God is with me, is He not?"

Darcie nodded, but didn't say a word. God. She wasn't sure she saw Him in any of this, or in much of anything. Not since she'd lost Haley in a freak car crash.

Pilar gestured at the iPad. "And it is wonderful that you have loaned me your iPad. You and Detective Noah have been so generous. I have saved my money and will be able to get a new computer soon." Gratitude shone on her face. "Detective Noah has even promised to help me find a quality computer for a good price."

"Are you ever going to start calling him just plain Noah?"

"Just plain Noah is much longer than Detective Noah, I think." She chuckled. "But no, I will continue to use Detective with him just as I call you Nurse Darcie. It is my way of showing my respect."

"We don't need that, Pilar. We know you respect us and our work. In fact, I wish you would stop. At least with me."

"Then I will."

"I have to go to the bathroom," Isabel announced from where she sat watching television.

Pilar started to move as if she planned to get up to help Isabel.

"Don't even think about it," Darcie warned. She squeezed Pilar's shoulder to soften the admonition and looked down into her eyes ringed with dark circles. Assuming the care for an injured young child was taking its toll on Pilar. She wouldn't admit it or complain at all. She loved Isabel and was thankful to have custody of her granddaughter, who'd lived many years with Mayte in terrible conditions.

Darcie firmly clasped the handles of Isabel's wheelchair, not caring that the pressure smarted against her skin. She'd rather be in pain than think about the callout where she'd found Isabel living in a squalid apartment with drug paraphernalia all around.

Darcie's anger from that day came roaring back. How could a mother treat her child like that? How could Mayte even have a child when Darcie's precious Haley been taken from her?

No, stop. It does no good.

What was the point in doing so? She'd asked these questions over and over, year after year, and God never answered. She'd concentrate on what she could do. Like spend even more time with Isabel to give Pilar a break.

Darcie wheeled Isabel into the bathroom and helped her maneuver the ankle-to-hip cast weighing her down. Darcie settled Isabel in place, then turned her back to give her privacy. Maybe for Darcie to get her emotions under control, too.

She took deep breaths like she'd done daily after Haley had died. Darcie couldn't save her own daughter, but she'd saved Isabel and could help improve her quality of life.

Darcie closed her eyes. Envisioned a happy place. A nice home for Pilar and Isabel, free from guns and gangs. Even Mayte could live there when she came out of rehab. Darcie imagined a cute little house in the sun. White with blue trim. A garden for Pilar. A swing set for Isabel. Birds chirping. Butterflies floating overhead. Maybe a rainbow or two.

A knock sounded on the door to Pilar's room. Darcie jumped and spun. Noah's deep voice soon rumbled through the space.

Noah. It's just Noah.

She blew out a breath. She'd been expecting him and was honestly glad he was here. She felt safer with him around. Far safer. But that wasn't good. She couldn't let herself depend on him or want him in her life for any reason.

"I'm done, Darcie," Isabel announced.

The innocence of the little girl's voice instantly replaced Darcie's thoughts with a smile. She helped Isabel wash her hands and get back into the chair, then stole a quick hug, drawing in the fresh scent of her strawberry shampoo. She loved the feel of the trusting child offering uncomplicated love and affection.

"Can we go see Noah?" she asked, her expression excited.

"Of course." Darcie wheeled her into Pilar's room.

"I'm glad you came," Isabel said.

"I'm glad to see you, too." Noah flashed a smiled but then stepped toward Darcie.

His worried expression set her anxiety flaring up again.

"Can I talk to you alone for a minute?" he asked.

Darcie's gut cramped hard, but she fought back the panic and looked at Pilar. "Will you two be okay if I step into the hallway for a few minutes?"

"Yes, of course," Pilar said, but her brow was tight with concern.

Darcie strode into a hallway similar to the ones she'd walked in during her years as a nurse. Noah moved close enough for a whiff of his spicy aftershave to overcome the familiar hospital smells. Close enough to see the small dimple in his cheek that always appeared when he smiled.

Ignore it. Ignore him. Ignore the desire to let him hold you and chase all your troubles away.

Ignore. Ignore. Ignore.

She would forever be in his debt for his help. She was also thankful he continued to help Isabel and Pilar, too. Darcie was able to handle a few hours here or there in his company while they focused on helping someone else. But now…now there would be an investigation into her attack. How was she going to avoid him as she'd tried to do since they'd met? To avoid the chemistry that always sparked between them?

She wasn't about to follow her interest and risk her heart again. Not with him. Not with any man. Not after losing her precious Haley and then her ex-husband, Tom, when he abandoned her after he was unable to deal with his grief. She'd once believed the people she loved could help her deal with life's trials. Believed that God could banish problems. But now she knew everything in her life depended on her and her alone.

She might be physically attracted to Noah, but it would go no further. He couldn't chase away her troubles. She was the only one who could do that.

She cut off her thoughts with a finely honed self-discipline she'd developed since Haley's death and faced him.

"I'm sorry, Darcie." He shoved a hand into his hair, leaving short little tufts standing at attention. "We tried our best, but we weren't able to apprehend the shooter."

Darcie's heart sank, but she didn't speak. Couldn't speak. What could she say after hearing the man who'd tried to kill her was still running free?

Noah pulled out a small notepad and a pen. "I got a quick look at the suspect's size and body type, but I'm hoping you can give me a facial description so I can put out an alert. Then you can meet with the sketch artist first thing in the morning."

Darcie forced herself to replay the details of her attack so she could describe the creep. "He was dark-skinned. Latino. His face was round, and he had stubble covering his chin. Maybe a full goatee—I'm not sure. He was mean-looking, Noah. So mean. Like he'd done this before. Killed someone, I mean." The fear that had nearly taken her down during the attack resurfaced, and she looked at Noah for a moment to take comfort from his warmth. His concern.

She jerked her gaze away before she started thinking she could continue to go to him for reassurance. Turning her head sent pain shooting through her tender neck, and her near-death experience came flashing back with a vengeance. Shivers started at her head, racing down her body like a rushing river. A cry of despair slipped out before she could stifle it.

"Hey." Noah stepped closer and rested a warm hand on her arm. "It's okay. You're safe."

Was she? Would this creep think she could identify him and come looking for her? Come after her with his gun, or even worse, try to strangle her again?

A full-on shudder claimed her body, and despite her efforts to fight back her tears, they started flowing. She tried to stop them, willed them away, but to no avail.

"Aw, no. Don't cry." Noah's arms went around her and he drew her close.

She'd forgotten the feel of a man's embrace other than from a friend, the warmth and tenderness, and she moved even closer, sobbing hard and soaking his shirt. She willingly reveled in his warmth and pushed to the recesses of her mind all thoughts of why allowing him to care for her was wrong.

She needed him. Just now. Not later. Never again. Just now.

He cradled her head and held her. Minute after minute. Standing strong. His arms enveloping her. Her fear receding. Calm returning and, along with it, her common sense. She allowed herself a few more moments to accept Noah's compassion that eased the chill from her heart, but when her tears fully subsided, she couldn't find an excuse to stay in his arms so she freed herself and looked up at him.

"Better?" he asked, his gaze tender as he pressed a wayward strand of hair behind her ear.

She didn't know how to reply and silence hung heavy between them. She should fill the quiet with words, with something, but she didn't want to admit that outside of his arms she felt afraid. If she did, he would insist on protecting her and that wouldn't be good for either of them. Nor would she lie and say she was okay.

She opted to simply take another step back and ignore his question. "Do you think my attacker will try to finish what he started?"

"If he thinks you can identify him, yes." Frowning, Noah flipped a page in his notebook. "If the attack was random—just you being in the wrong place at the wrong time—then there's a good chance he won't know where to find you. But there's always the possibility that he specifically targeted you. If that's the case, then he might know your name or how to track you down. Have you thought of a possible motive for the attack?"

"Motive? No. I have no idea who he is or why he did this. He was just suddenly there, behind me, grabbing me around the throat." She touched her neck, feeling the tenderness.

Noah ground his teeth for a moment. "Do you think the attack could be related to your work? Like maybe you treated a guy on one of your ambulance runs, and he's mad at you for some reason?"

"It's possible, I suppose." She paused to think about it. "I see people when they're in crisis. Sometimes it sets them off, but to attack me for it? Seems far-fetched. And I don't remember a patient who looks like him, but maybe." She shrugged. "I treat so many people in a day…"

"Still, I'm thinking you'd remember someone mad enough to want to kill you."

"I hope so. If I don't, I'm not very in tune with the care they need. Which likely means this isn't related to work."

He jotted a note on his pad. "I'll still request a list of your callouts for the last few weeks, and we'll start there."

"We?" she asked, the word fighting its way up her throat. "You're going to be working this case?"

"The jerk was shooting to kill. He'll be charged with attempted murder and that falls within homicide's purview." He studied her, his eyes a piercing gray instead of the usual muted blue. "Is that a problem?"

Of course it is. On a personal level. But what about the professional? It was a blessing to have a top Portland detective working this investigation. "I'm sure you'll do a great job."

He shoved his notebook into his pocket. "I'll get the description out to patrol, then escort you home. If I know your squad, they'll want to hear the whole story, and you can give me your full statement then."

"Whole story? You think they'll stop at that? They're going to want to see the forensic evidence, too." Despite her ongoing fear, the thought of her teammates having her back made her smile. "And they'll hound you during this investigation to make sure you're doing everything you can to bring this guy in. So be prepared."

"No worries there." His expression sobered. "I won't stop until this creep is behind bars."

The dedication in his voice surprised her, and she didn't know how to respond so she simply stared at him. As if embarrassed at the emotions he'd displayed, he suddenly spun and pushed open Pilar's door.

At the sound of Isabel's voice, Darcie grabbed Noah's arm. "Wait."

He turned, his hand resting on the slightly open door. "What is it?"

"Since you've been helping with Isabel you should know that Isabel and Pilar will be staying with me in my condo."

His eyes narrowed. "Are you sure that's a good idea?"

"The condo is small and we'll be a little cramped, but with the gunshot wound Pilar can't care for Isabel so I'll be taking over."

"I'm not talking about the accommodations." He made strong eye contact. "Since we know nothing about the shooter, this incident could be related to your relationship with Pilar and Isabel."

"Pilar and Isabel? How?"

"Mayte may be in rehab, but she still has deep connections with the drug world." He scrubbed a hand over his face as if the thought made him weary. "Based on the clothing the suspect wore, I wouldn't be surprised if he was a gangster, and you know that means drugs. They could be trying to send a warning to Mayte."

Darcie swiveled to look through the open doorway at Isabel. If this incident was related to her mother's past, it was an even more compelling reason to put Isabel under the protection of the FRS at the restored firehouse where they all lived together. No matter what Noah said or thought.

Darcie widened her stance and planted her feet

as she often did with unruly patients to let them know she was in charge. "Pilar has to spend the night here, but Isabel *will* be coming home with me today and I *will* pick up Pilar tomorrow."

Noah released the door and stepped close enough that she could see slivers of black mixing with the gray in his eyes. "Let me be clear about this, Darcie, so you know the risk. If we're dealing with gangbangers, they won't care who gets in the way. Bringing Isabel and Pilar home with you could put you and the whole FRS team in danger."

He spoke the truth, but what else could she do? She didn't want to put her coworkers—her friends—in danger, but if she presented her case to them, she knew they'd all agree with her decision.

She reaffirmed her stance. "You know as well as I do that everyone on the team puts the lives and safety of others first. They'll risk a little danger to protect an innocent child and her grandmother and none of them will even bat a lash."

THREE

Noah paced the communal living area on the first floor of the team's remodeled firehouse. Upper floors of the historic building held individual condos for the team members, while the kitchen, dining room and game room were available to them on the main level. Kerr Development once owned the historic building and had it slated to be sold until Darcie saved Winnie Kerr's life on a callout. Winnie was so grateful for Darcie's care and ensuing friendship that she remodeled the firehouse as a home for the entire FRS. She donated the building to the county, along with an endowment that allowed the team to live there rent-free. A sweet deal for all of them.

Tonight all of the team members and their significant others had gathered for a group dinner, but Darcie's attack changed everything. They'd put dinner on hold and waited for Darcie to provide details of the assault after she took Isabel upstairs for a nap.

Noah had to give the team credit. They'd restrained their natural instinct to take charge and go barreling out the door to find Darcie's attacker right away. Any one of them, from team leader Jake Marsh, to sniper Brady Owens, bomb expert Cash Dixon, or negotiators Skyler Hunter and Archer Reed, were capable of mounting a hunt for Darcie's attacker. Instead, they'd patiently sat in wait. Maybe it had to do with the addition of Skyler's husband, or Brady's and Cash's fiancées to the group. Maybe they served as a calming influence on the high-strung team.

Brady suddenly shot to his feet. He never sat still for long and had been whittling away on a chunk of wood, the shavings piling up near his feet. "How long does it take to get a kid to sleep?"

"Cut her some slack, honey." His fiancée, Morgan, looked up from where she perched on the arm of the chair he'd occupied. "After Isabel's scare, Darcie likely wants to be sure she's sound asleep before leaving her alone."

"I know, but—" He dropped back into the chair.

Morgan pressed a finger against his lips and

surprisingly, he smiled up at her and didn't argue, but fell silent.

Looked like Noah's take on the significant others was on target.

Footsteps sounded above, then Noah heard the click of shoes coming down the stairway. He crossed the room to see Darcie slowly descend. She was long and lean, with legs that didn't seem to quit. She'd changed out of her work uniform of black pants and polo shirt into jeans and a bright blue sweater with a high collar. The color highlighted the generous red tint to her hair, something he'd often thought was related to her fiery personality. And the neckline covered the bruises on her throat—a choice that he figured was probably deliberate.

"You poor thing." Cash's fiancée, Krista, rushed over to Darcie and led her toward an open chair as if she was a fragile teacup. "I can't imagine having a guy try to choke me. And bullets? I'd faint."

Morgan joined them, her blond hair standing out in contrast to the dark-headed pair. She patted Darcie's shoulder, then squatted next to her. "It's terrible. Just terrible. What can we do to help?"

Darcie shrank back from their enthusiastic concern. She started turning a small silver ring around and around on her pinkie finger. The ring had belonged to her daughter, Haley, and Noah knew she played with it when she was nervous. She hated being the center of attention like this and rarely let people focus on her. She usually sidestepped questions about her life and her past, but the attack seemed to have rattled her more than she was letting on, as she simply stared into the distance.

"This is crazy," Noah said, purposefully pulling the attention from her.

"What is?" Krista pushed her hair from her face to look up at him.

Noah forced a lighthearted tone to his voice. "For the first time ever, someone is mothering Darcie instead of her taking them under her wing."

"Noah's right." Jake Marsh smiled down on Darcie from where he stood by the blazing fireplace, his stance wide and ready for action, as usual. Jake was tough and in charge, but Noah also knew how much he cared and that he would put his own life on the line for his team members.

"Guess it's a side benefit of having more women around." Cash smiled up at Krista, and Noah couldn't help but gape. The former Army Ranger and bomb tech seemed to have mellowed out, too.

"What does that say about me, then?" Skyler got up and stared at Cash. Petite, with curly red hair, she was a lot tougher than her pint-sized stature made her seem. And she was one of the finest negotiators and detectives Noah had ever met.

"Don't take offense, sweetheart." Logan claimed his wife's hand. "You have a heart of gold, but most of the time you're more in a round up criminals and take names' kind of mode."

Noah expected Skyler to get mad, and he waited for her response.

She wrinkled her nose. "I kind of am, aren't I?"

Logan smiled fondly at Skyler. "As an FBI agent, I appreciate that, as do your teammates. Krista and Morgan, on the other hand…?"

"Hey." Morgan snapped her head up. "Don't put words in our mouths. We like Skyler just fine, don't we, Krista?"

"Well." Krista's face suddenly lit with mischief. "Maybe she could shrink an inch so I'm not the shortest person in the group, but yeah, otherwise she's great."

Skyler scowled in mock offense and the teammates broke out in laughter. Even Darcie smiled, once again proving to Noah that this team acted more like family than coworkers. Darcie was blessed to be a part of the group. He wished he had the same thing on the job, but most of the guys he hung with were married and focused on their own families, and he was like a fifth wheel.

And his real family? They hadn't spoken much since they'd learned about Ashley. About his son, Evan. Her parents had raised the baby and they wouldn't let his parents anywhere near their only grandson. Noah deserved their reproach, but it stung. And to make matters worse, they'd recently learned that Evan wasn't brought up in the Christian faith. It weighed heavy on Noah's mind, night and day. And put a boatload of guilt in his heart, too.

"I may not be the soft and squishy type," Skyler said, transferring her focus to Darcie, "but I can make a mean cup of tea. I'll get you one." She went straight to the adjoining kitchen.

Jake dropped into a recliner and pushed it back, his focus locked on Darcie. "Noah gave us the basics of your attack, but I'd like to hear about it in your own words."

Her face blanched. Noah grabbed onto the fireplace mantel to keep from crossing over to her to offer comfort. Not only wasn't it a good idea, but she'd also hate the extra attention.

Krista took Darcie's hand. "Take your time, sweetie. I understand. I'll never forget the creep who tried to kill me, but it gets easier to deal with as time passes. I promise."

Noah had heard something about Krista's abduction six months ago when Cash had saved her life, but Noah didn't know more than that.

Darcie extracted her hand, leaned back in her chair and started in on the details of her attack. She described the suspect and her breathing intensified as tears started to form. She was a strong woman, but even strong women cried after a harrowing attack, and it was going to take Darcie time to get over the experience.

Her voice faltered and she blinked hard. "I don't know this creep, but Noah wonders if it's related to someone from a callout who didn't like the way I treated him."

Brady scoffed. "I expect you'd nearly have to kill someone to cause this extreme reaction. Anyone whose care you botched lately?"

"Brady," Morgan scolded. "I'm sure there's a more delicate way to ask."

Brady smiled at her. It wasn't hard to see he was head over heels in love with the woman. "Never claimed there was anything delicate about me, honey."

"Subtlety was never Brady's strong suit." Archer grinned at Morgan. "And you're the one who chose to get engaged to the guy. We inherited him."

"Thanks a lot." Brady fake slugged Archer's arm.

Archer laughed. "No problem, man. What are friends for?"

"Focus, people," Jake interrupted, to keep the

team on task. "Darcie, can you think of anyone who might want to retaliate—not because you did anything wrong in their care, but because they just weren't happy with the results? Someone who was left permanently disabled, maybe?"

She shook her head. "I've been thinking about it since Noah mentioned it, and I'm coming up blank."

"I've already got my team pulling the callout records from dispatch," Noah offered. "But I'm also wondering if this is gang-related."

"Gang." Jake sat forward, slamming down his leg rest and fixing his gaze on Noah. "How so?"

"This is just a hunch, mind you. I didn't get a close look at the shooter, but he wore Nuevo gang colors. And we all know about the gang problems in that neighborhood."

"Never heard of the Nuevo gang," Cash said.

"They're a recently formed offshoot of another faction. Nuevo means new. Hence the name."

Darcie frowned. "But I'm not involved with or connected to a gang."

"Regardless," Noah replied, "I'll talk to our detective on the metro gang task force to see if he has any thoughts on the attack."

"I don't like this uncertainty." Morgan twisted her hands. "There's got to be a connection to narrow this down. Or how else will we know whether or not everyone here is in danger?"

"This isn't related to the team, is it?" Krista shot a questioning look at Noah.

"Maybe," he said. "But I think it's less likely than some of the other options."

Jake narrowed his gaze. "Could be related to the Vargas family."

"The Vargas family?" Krista asked.

"He's talking about Isabel, Mayte and Pilar." Skyler came back into the room carrying a mug of steaming tea. She handed it to Darcie and grinned. "Is this where I should give you a hug or something?"

Darcie returned the smile, and Noah liked seeing the change in her attitude even if it was just for the moment. "I'm good for now."

"Morgan's right, you know," Brady said. "If this is related to the squad we need to know."

Noah opened his mouth to speak, but the team started tossing out thoughts on possible suspects. No point in fighting to be heard. He leaned back and listened, but he kept his eye on Darcie, who sipped her tea and said very little.

"Back to the Vargas family," Jake said. "Could this have something to do with Mayte's drug habit?"

"I wondered the same thing," Noah admitted. "I'll start looking in to that, too."

"You're heading up this investigation, then?" Archer asked.

Noah nodded and waited for one of them to ask about his credentials and if PPB had a more qualified detective.

"So there's no clear reason for the attack." Logan weighed in for the first time. "Did you ever consider it's just a random attack? Maybe a robbery?"

"I thought of that," Darcie said. "But if all he wanted was my money, why didn't he pull his gun and demand my purse instead of trying to choke me to death?"

"Good point. It does sound more like someone wanted you dead." Logan frowned. "Odd that he'd attempt it out in broad daylight like that with witnesses around."

"If he *is* a gangster," Noah said, "the locals are so afraid of the gangs, they'd never testify against them, so the gangsters don't bother trying to hide. And, honestly, the attack in broad daylight is right in line with a gangster's behavior."

Archer nodded. "They aren't known for their subtlety."

Jake was still frowning. "Until we can prove a connection to a gang, we'll need to explore all other possibilities."

Brady leveled his gaze at Darcie. "You've never really talked about your ex. Could he be behind this?"

Darcie's mouth fell open for a second, before she snapped it closed and took a deep breath. "Tom doesn't have any gang ties."

Brady leaned forward. "He could have hired someone."

"He's right, Darcie," Skyler said. "I know Tom came to see you a few weeks ago. He seemed pretty angry when he left. Could it be related to that?"

Darcie opened her mouth, then closed it again and looked down at her hands. "We own a house together from when we were married. He wants to sell it. Says he needs the money. I'm not ready to let it go."

"I know you don't want to think he could harm you, but money or the lack thereof, is a powerful motivator," Archer said.

"I should probably look in to him." Noah tried to sound like it would be an unpleasant thing to do, when truth was, he hoped to learn more about Darcie in the process since she shared little about her personal life.

"Do what you have to do," she said, but didn't look up.

Archer shifted in his chair. "Has anyone thought about Winnie Kerr's sons?"

"The woman who donated this place?" Morgan asked.

Archer nodded. "She recently changed her

will, cutting out her sons and leaving Darcie a sizable inheritance. Her sons didn't like it and they're trying to prove Winnie's not of sound mind."

Darcie lifted her head, sorrow lingering in her expression. "I'm scheduled to testify on Winnie's behalf."

"Sounds like a good motive for murder." Archer swung his gaze to Noah. "Since this is a financial lead and I have an MBA, mind if I do a bit of checking on it for you? Would help relieve some of your workload."

"I'm glad for the help." Noah handed a business card to Archer. "Keep me updated on your progress."

"And you'll do the same thing," Jake demanded, his focus fixed squarely on Noah's face.

Noah didn't like sharing confidential information outside of his department, but there was no point in arguing with Jake. He'd get the information somehow, so Noah might as well provide it. He nodded his agreement.

Darcie set down her teacup and stood. "I don't know about the rest of you, but I'm tired of talking about this. It's my night to cook dinner, and it's time for me to get started."

"Oh, honey." Morgan jumped up. "You don't need to cook. We can do it."

Darcie gave a firm shake of her head, then

winced. Noah suspected it was from the bruises he'd seen before she hid them under her sweater. "Making dinner will keep my mind busy."

With her shoulders back, she turned and marched to the kitchen, looking like the resolute, amazing woman Noah knew her to be. After losing her daughter and then her marriage, she'd clawed her way back to normalcy in her life, but Noah knew it had been a long, hard struggle. He also knew if such a tragedy didn't keep her down, nothing would.

The problem was, in an effort to keep up a strong act or to fight through her fears, she could very well ignore the danger she was in and do something foolish. It was just one of many things that would keep Noah on alert until he apprehended her attacker.

FOUR

Alone at last in the kitchen, Darcie planted her hands on the granite countertop, her back to the family room. The cool, smooth surface took the sting out of her hands. She needed time to process this day. Time away from everyone else. She couldn't rush up to her condo for fear of waking Isabel, so she'd gone with the first thought that had come into her head—the kitchen.

Unfortunately, it was open to the family room, leaving her in full view. Still, cooking for this many people was a big job and no one on the squad would offer to help when it wasn't their night, so she should have the kitchen all to herself. It was sweet of Morgan to offer to take over, but when Darcie pushed the point, Morgan certainly hadn't insisted.

Fighting down a panic attack, one like the many she'd experienced after Haley died and Tom bailed on her, Darcie set to work on her family's simple shrimp-boil recipe. She dug out a large stockpot and started water flowing. She unearthed several pounds of fresh shrimp, plump sausage and ears of corn from the refrigerator, then found a bag of baby red potatoes in the bin. As she retrieved the spice boiling bags from the pantry, Noah stepped into the room.

He smiled, but she could see he was testing her mood. "What are you making?"

"Shrimp boil—shrimp, corn on the cob, sausage and red potatoes all cooked with seafood spices," she answered, trying to sound calm and collected so he would think she'd recovered from the attack and go home.

"You probably ate a lot of seafood growing up in Florida."

"Yes," she said.

"Do you go back there often?"

"Not really." The fact that her family had disowned her when she married Tom, who was nothing more than an unemployed biker when they met, had nothing to do with the investigation, so she didn't bring it up.

"Want some help?"

"No."

"Are you sure?"

She sighed and met his gaze. "Look, Noah, I don't want you to think I'm not grateful for your help today, but if this is your way of getting me to talk about the incident and how I'm feeling, I'm done with that and ready to move on."

"I'm that obvious, am I?" He grinned and his dimple, the one that seemed to beg her to poke a finger into it, appeared.

Instead, she turned off the water and started the gas burner beneath the pot.

"I'd hoped to talk to you about reviewing your callout list," he continued. "I'm sure it's in my email by now and we can sit down to review it together."

She turned to him. "Tonight?"

"Yes, if you're up to it."

She had the stamina and the desire to do it tonight, but having Noah in her home made her think about him as a man and not a police detective. She didn't need that distraction right now when her focus should be on helping him find her attacker. "I'm glad to work on the investigation with you at the precinct. We could do it in the morning right after I finish with the sketch artist."

He watched her for a moment, a cloud darkening his eyes, then he shrugged and seemed to relax.

"So what you're saying is I'm not invited to dinner," he joked, but she could hear the hurt behind his words.

She looked up at him. "Do you think it's a good idea for you to stay?"

"You mean because you're cooking?" That grin again and the dimple. She could barely resist the dimple.

She sighed.

"Okay, sorry," he said sincerely. "I'm afraid you're going to have to get used to spending time with me as I'm not leaving you alone until your attacker is caught."

She crossed her arms. "I won't be alone. I have the team."

"A team who could be called out at any time of the day or night."

"I'd go with them on the callout, then."

"You'd have to stay here to care for Isabel. You really don't want me to leave the two of you alone, do you?"

No. Yes. "I have a gun."

He eyed her. "That you're not willing to use."

Her shoulders went up defensively. "I might have shot him."

"Maybe," he said, keeping his probing gaze fixed on her. "When's the last time you went to the range to practice your marksmanship?"

A few months, but she wouldn't tell him that. She shrugged.

He planted his hands on the counter. "Then

after we get through the callout list tomorrow, we'll be heading to the range."

"You don't need—"

"I know I don't need to take you to the range." He crossed his arms and put on his serious detective expression, which made him look hard and unyielding. Annoyingly, she found it equally as attractive as the cute dimple. "Anyone on the team can take you, or you could go on your own. But since I'm the one who has the problem with not letting you out of my sight until this guy is caught, you'll humor me and let me see how well you can handle a gun." He held her gaze, issuing her a challenge.

She thought to argue, but she knew he'd stand right there and keep at her until she agreed with him. She liked his tenacity. His strength and determination. Just not when he directed it at her.

"Now, I'm inviting myself to dinner." He waved a hand over the counter. "What do you need help with?" He jutted out his chin as if challenging her to tell him he wasn't wanted.

She was done fighting him for the night. After the attack, she had no energy left to do battle over something like this. "Do you know how to shuck corn on the cob?"

At the instant brightening of his mood, she regretted her decision to let him stay.

"No, but I'm sure you can teach me."

She slid the bag of corn across the island. "It's not hard. Cut off both ends and start peeling off the outer husk, then the silk strings. If the silk is stubborn try running it under water."

She turned her back on him before he asked for additional directions. She went to the sink and started peeling the shrimp. She felt him watching her every move and resisted sighing for about the zillionth time today.

She'd always thought if they argued the spark between them would ignite into something fierce. It had and they were about to spend time together. Maybe a lot of it. Could they do so without the tension mounting every second? If not, she'd be in world of hurt by the time they captured the shooter.

Noah got up from the dining table and carried his plate to the kitchen. From everyone's reactions, he was sure that dinner had been amazing, but the tender shrimp had felt like sawdust in his mouth, and he'd had to choke it down. His fault. Totally. He'd gotten his feelings hurt. There, he admitted it. How girlie was that? He was supposed to be this tough cop and he'd let Darcie hurt his feelings when she'd made it clear that she wanted him to leave.

So what had he done about it? Invited himself to dinner. Dumb. Really dumb. He could have just sat outside and kept an eye on the house. He didn't need the added pain of being in Darcie's company when he wasn't wanted.

He shook his head, hoping to erase the memory of the tense meal, where her team members kept casting him and Darcie long looks. They knew there were sparks between the two of them. They were law enforcement officers with finely honed observation skills, so how could they not see it? Even Logan, who was new to the group, got it. Krista and Morgan were the only ones who seemed to be in the dark.

He set his plate on the counter next to the pile of dishes everyone ditched before moving to the family room. Darcie insisted on cleaning up, too, saying it was her responsibility and she wasn't going to shirk it.

Noah heard the television news playing in the family room. He should go see what the reporters were saying about the shooting. Instead, he watched Darcie load the dishwasher. Despite the fiasco at dinner and his brain warning him to back off, he couldn't seem to keep his eyes off her.

Look at him. Standing there like a fool after a dinner that nearly made him hurl. If a chance to have dinner here came up in the future, he'd say no, even *if* it was his last meal on earth and eating here was his only choice. He'd take hunger, thank you very much.

His phone rang and he looked at the screen. His lieutenant.

"Lockhart," he answered and leaned against the island.

"Thought you'd like to know we completed our canvass and forensics finished their sweep." Emerson's tone was flat, as if he didn't care about the outcome.

"And?" Noah asked, hoping they'd located a lead on their shooter.

"The canvass didn't turn anything up. Several people were either not home or not willing to open their door to us. You know how it goes. They may have seen something, may even know the guy, but they're not going to help."

Noah wished he didn't know how that went. They'd solve more cases if people spoke up. "It's not surprising for that neighborhood."

"Exactly. I'll have officers follow up and let you know if they convince anyone to break their silence."

"And the criminalists? They find any forensic evidence?"

"Yeah, but you're not going to like it."

"Go ahead." Noah gritted his teeth.

"They recovered a crumpled piece of paper with Darcie Stevens's name on it. It was located where the shooter vaulted over the fence. Like he was trying to ditch it in case he got caught."

"Darcie's name's on it?" he repeated like a parrot.

She must have heard him as she pivoted to look at him.

"See for yourself," Emerson said. "I'll text a photo of it to you right now."

After drawing Darcie's attention, Noah decided not to ask any additional questions before getting a look at the picture. His phone dinged and he opened the file. The scrap of paper held a handwritten list with the numbers one through three and a name listed behind each number. First place belonged to Leland King, second to Ramon Flores. Bright red slashes ran through each of their names. Darcie's name took the third slot. Slash-free.

A hit list.

FIVE

Noah was unable to formulate words to continue his conversation with his lieutenant. The more Noah looked at the picture, the more he was sure it was a hit list. And Darcie was the only one left to kill. She'd be dead already if she hadn't gotten free from her attacker.

Acid churned up Noah's throat and he swallowed hard as he lifted the phone to his mouth.

"If there was any question that the attack on Stevens was random," Emerson continued, "there's no question anymore."

Noah wanted to slam a fist into the wall. To do anything but stand there emotionless. But he didn't want to tell Darcie about the list until he had a moment to process the news. "Has anyone had a chance to check out the other two names?"

"It just landed on my desk, so no. I thought you'd want first crack at it."

"You've got that right." Noah studied the names. "Maybe we're reading too much into this and the list is just a reminder for the dude to call them."

"Seriously, Lockhart. You take a trip on the Alice in Wonderland express or something? You know as well as I do that the gangsters who live in that neighborhood don't keep notes to remind themselves to call people. It's a hit list, and once you process this lead, you're gonna discover the men on the list are already dead."

"I know." Noah wished he could say something to the contrary.

Emerson was silent for a long time. "This personal thing with Stevens that we talked about earlier. Is it getting in the way of your objectivity, Lockhart? 'Cause if it is, I'll pull you from this case so fast your head will spin."

"No, sir," Noah replied even though he suspected it already had. "I'm good."

"See that it stays that way and keep me in the loop on your progress." Emerson disconnected.

Darcie came over and stood next to him. "What is it?"

He wanted to shield her from the truth, but she had a right to know. He held out his phone.

She stared at the screen, then looked up with narrowed eyes. "What is that?"

"A list found in the forensic sweep of the area where the shooter went over the fence."

She returned to staring at the screen. "But who are these men?"

"You don't recognize the names?"

"No. So why am I on a list with them and why are they crossed—" Her head shot up. "Oh, no! It's a hit list, isn't it?"

"Likely," he said reluctantly.

"And these guys are already dead, right?"

"I don't know, but that's what I aim to find out." He pushed off the counter and shoved the phone into his pocket. "Jake mentioned at dinner that he isn't on call and will be here all night, so I'll head into the office and get started running their names."

"Wait." She grabbed his arm. "Can't you do it here? You can use our computer in the office."

"You want me here?'

"Yes. Please."

"When it suits you, all of a sudden you want me to stay," he said before he could stop the words from coming out of his mouth.

A hurt look flashed over her face and she backed up. "I want to know what you find out the minute you find it out. If that means you stay here to work, then that's what I want."

He opened his mouth to reply, but she held up a hand.

"I know that sounds cold and like I'm using

you, but I'll do just about anything to find out why this man is trying to kill me."

Noah wanted to refuse her. To march out the door and not come back, but he could never say no to those large brown eyes pleading with him, or ignore the concern for her safety that made his gut hurt. "I'll get my laptop from the car."

He didn't wait for her response, but headed for the front door. Outside, he let the icy wind coming from the north slap him in the face and cool his emotions. Emotions that had risen to the surface again. No surprise. Darcie did that to him.

So what? He was a grown man and could certainly wrangle down some feelings to get the job done. He grabbed his computer and vowed not to let her get to him again.

Back in the house, she escorted him to an office behind the family room and opened a desk drawer to retrieve a paper with the Wi-Fi log-in details.

She handed the paper to him and went to the door. "Make yourself at home. After I finish in the kitchen, I'll be in the family room if you need anything. Will you please come tell me when you've discovered something?"

He set his laptop on the tidy desk. "This could take some time, you know. Are you sure you want me to hang around that long?"

"I said whatever it takes and I mean it. I'll be

in the family room when you're ready to talk to me." She started to leave, then looked back. "One good thing about the list. At least it rules out my ex, right?"

"Would seem to, unless he's suddenly gotten into the business of hiring a hit man to kill people," Noah joked.

She smiled weakly. "For what it's worth, he and I ended things badly, but he's not a bad man. He's certainly not a killer and I really think looking into him would have been a waste of time." She took off before Noah could tell her he still had to investigate Tom. Any good detective would start with the people closest to the victim. But tonight, he'd focus on Ramon Flores and Leland King.

He dropped into a leather desk chair and connected to the database to begin searching for the men. His local search didn't take long and he came up empty. Wouldn't stop him. He widened the area. Took him about an hour, but he'd discovered three Leland Kings in three different cities in Oregon, but still no Ramon Flores.

He leaned back and clasped his hands behind his head. He had to come up with a game plan to find these guys and do so quickly.

Skyler came to the door and leaned against the jamb. Her expression was clear and guileless, so he didn't think Darcie was trying to avoid him by sending her teammate to check in.

"How's the investigation going?" she asked.

He stretched his arms overhead, working out the kinks in his back from hunching over the computer. "Wish I could report having found something, but nothing much so far."

A spark that Noah recognized from his years as a detective lit Skyler's eyes. County couldn't afford a fulltime FRS, meaning each team member performed other duties for the county when they weren't on a callout. Skyler's secondary assignment was as a Special Investigations Unit detective.

"Mind sharing what you've got?" she asked, that gleam growing.

"I'd be glad to have another opinion." He motioned to a chair on the other side of the desk. "I suppose Darcie told you about the note we found on the scene."

"No, she didn't mention it." Skyler dropped into the chair. "I love Darcie to death, but she's not one to share. Prying into and fixing other people's lives, on the other hand, are things that she's a master at."

"Then maybe I should wait until she tells you."

"It would be better for Darcie if I don't have to question her about this." Skyler settled back in the chair, proving she wasn't going anywhere.

She was right. He could spare Darcie from having to talk about the hit list. He gave Skyler a quick recap and asked her to keep it between them. "I've been running both names through the databases. I've located three men named Leland King in Oregon, none in the Portland area. And nothing on Flores."

"If this is a gang thing, Flores could be an illegal."

"Meaning I won't find anything in here." He jabbed a thumb at his computer. "I was already planning to call the metro-gang task force in the morning. I'll just add this to the conversation."

"I'm off tomorrow. I could run down the three Kings."

"Run down the kings? Good one." He chuckled.

She arched a questioning brow.

"Don't you see it?" he asked, still smiling. "The three kings with their gifts of gold, frankincense and myrrh. You running them down."

She rolled her eyes.

"Okay," he said, letting the humor go. "I'd be glad for your help."

She stood. "I'll get back to you the minute I find anything."

"One more thing," Noah said. "I know over dinner we nearly exhausted every possibility of who might want to kill Darcie, but you're the person closest to her. Do you think the ex-husband could be involved in this?"

Skyler shrugged. "I know as much about Tom as you do. But with the hit list, Tom seems like a long shot to me." She paused and tapped a finger on her chin. "Still, you can't rule anything out at this point."

"No, I can't." And Darcie needed to know that.

Noah came to his feet, dreading the look on Darcie's face when he told her about his lack of success in here, and that striking out meant they'd still be reviewing the callout list together in the morning. That he'd follow up on Tom, too.

She wasn't going to like his news, but she'd said she'd do whatever it took to figure out why the shooter had come after her.

A strong statement. Too strong?

Maybe. He hoped by the time they sorted out this investigation and learned the shooter's identity, she wouldn't regret her words.

The morning air was crisp and cold, so Darcie slipped her jacket over an old turtleneck she'd paired with jeans, then stepped to the door of her condo. She grabbed the knob, groaned, then turned back. She caught Pilar watching her intently from the sofa. She'd been discharged first thing that morning, and Archer, who was off for a few days, had been kind enough to pick her up. Or maybe *kind* wasn't the right word. Archer was a kind guy, but he was more motivated by the idea of not letting Darcie leave the safety of the firehouse to get Pilar when he could do so for her.

"Did you forget something?" Pilar asked.

Darcie glanced at Isabel to see if she was listening, but her nose was in a book and she didn't even look up. Darcie shrugged out of her coat. "I decided to change clothes."

Pilar wrinkled her nose. "This is a good thing, I think. You look like you have run out of clean laundry and are on your way to wash your good clothing. Not at all like you are going to meet Detective Noah at his work."

Darcie felt warmth rush up her face. "Why didn't you say something at breakfast?"

"I thought you were going to change, but then you put on your jacket before I could mention it."

"Oh," Darcie said, feeling like a girl receiving advice from her mother. Not that Darcie had any experience with the sweet motherly tone coming from Pilar. Darcie's mother had never dispensed gentle advice. She'd just snapped out her commands and expected unconditional compliance.

"I'll just change." Darcie went to her room and selected a sweater and khaki pants that she'd tried on then promptly shed an hour ago. One of three different outfits lying on her bed that she'd considered after she'd told herself not to primp for her meeting with Noah. She'd finally gotten disgusted with herself for thinking so much about her clothing and decided to wear something that would make her look horrible. If Pilar's comment meant anything, Darcie had succeeded.

She took a quick look in the mirror. The neck of the sweater left the bruises that had darkened overnight visible. At the front door, she grabbed a scarf and gently knotted it over the purple and greenish blotches.

Pilar looked up. "Are you ever going to tell me about those bruises?"

Darcie pointed at Isabel. "Maybe when we're alone."

Pilar nodded, but Darcie knew the woman could see right through her. If Darcie had a living grandmother, she would want her to be as wonderful and plainspoken as Pilar. At least, most of the time.

Darcie slipped into her coat. "I don't know how long I'll be. There's plenty of food in the kitchen, and remember it's fine for Isabel to play in the game room. Archer will be here all day watching out for the two of you."

"He is a bit reserved, but I can tell he is a good man, is he not?"

Darcie liked Archer, but she found him the hardest teammate to get to know. She'd been on the team since its inception six years ago and Archer had been with them for three years. Still, Darcie didn't feel she knew him well. One reason was because of the trust fund from his family that ensured he'd never have to work another day in his life. Not that he lived off it or acted all snooty, but he was always wary of people, especially women, liking him for his money.

"Did I say something wrong?" Pilar asked.

Darcie realized she was frowning and forced out a smile. "It's not you and you're right. Archer is definitely one of the good guys."

Pilar struggled to her feet. She had arthritis in her knees, and she took her time crossing the room. She only came up to Darcie's chest and had to bend back to make eye contact.

"You are one of the good ones, too, Darcie. You are sent from God." She threw her pudgy arms around Darcie and hugged her hard. She smelled like the egg *chilaquiles* and strong coffee she'd prepared for breakfast. She stepped back. "And I know when the time is right, you will tell me about the bruises. I will not mention it again." She mimicked running a zipper over her lips.

Despite Pilar's insistence on prying when Darcie didn't want to share, she smiled fondly down on Pilar and squeezed her hand before leaving the condo. At the landing, she found Jake leaning against the wall, his phone in hand. Though Noah had wanted to pick her up, she'd asked Jake to give her a ride to Portland's central precinct to keep from spending any extra time alone with Noah.

Jake looked up. "Wondered if you were coming."

"Sorry, I was talking to Pilar." The truth, technically. No reason to mention how many times she'd changed clothes, like a teenage girl getting ready for a date.

They headed down the stairs at the same time as Archer stepped into the entryway. He glanced at his watch. "You should get going or you'll be late."

She wasn't one to stress over being on time, but Archer managed his schedule to the second. He'd gotten his MBA before he decided to become a deputy, and he often commented that time meant money.

The doorbell rang and Darcie jumped. She thought she'd come to grips with the attack. Guess she was wrong.

"You stay here with Jake. I'll see who it is." Archer went to the door, looked through the peephole and pulled open the door. "What are you doing here, Lockhart?"

Noah? She seconded Archer's surprise.

"Since I have to go downtown anyway, I thought I'd save Jake a trip. Is Darcie ready?" he asked, sounding like he was expected.

Why couldn't he have been a minute later, so she'd already be in the car with Jake? Now that he'd arrived, she couldn't justify wasting Jake's valuable time. She turned to him. "Thanks for offering to take me, but since Noah's here, I'll catch a ride with him."

He nodded. "Keep me informed of any developments."

Resolved to keep Noah at arm's length today, she stepped to the door and for a moment, she just stared at him. Under a leather jacket, he wore a plain black shirt tailored to his muscled body and paired it with black slacks, making him look dangerous. He was freshly showered and shaved, a smile on his face. That dimple winking at her.

How was she going to get through the day when the mere sight of him made her stand and stare like a dolt?

"I wasn't expecting you," she finally said, sounding like a total airhead.

His cool blue eyes told her he knew she was struggling. "Thought I'd help out."

"And I appreciate it, but next time a heads-up would be better." Her words came out testier than she'd intended.

"You're sure you don't want to ride with Jake?" Archer eyed Noah.

As a negotiator, Archer noticed subtle nuances and he had to be picking up on the tense vibe between her and Noah.

"I'm perfectly safe with Noah," she said, meaning her physical safety, of course. Mental and emotional were another story. "Call me if Pilar or Isabel need anything."

She stepped outside and stopped to prepare herself to spend time with Noah in the confines of a car where she couldn't simply walk away if the tension escalated between them. She looked up at the late winter sun shining through gray skies. Weak rays filtered down to the frosty grass, making it sparkle.

"No dallying." Noah took her arm and urged her to his car.

He opened the passenger door and she eyed him.

"Don't fight me on this, Darcie," he said with determination. "You're on a hit list. If they found you on your way to Pilar and Isabel's house, they can find you here, too."

The thought sent a tremor through her body and she felt for the weight of her gun in her purse.

As she slid into the car, she wished she'd taken her target practice with the team more seriously.

Noah settled behind the wheel and without a word merged into traffic. They'd driven for thirty minutes when he glanced at her. "Can you set up an appointment for me to talk to Winnie Kerr?"

"You mean for us," Darcie added. "I want to talk to her, too."

"For us, then. This afternoon if possible. I need to get her take on how your attack could be related to her will or her competency hearing."

Darcie grabbed her phone and made the call, but it turned out that Winnie was out of town. Darcie arranged a meeting time for when Winnie returned on Friday. Winnie rattled on about her niece and Darcie was glad to talk to her friend. Plus, it alleviated Darcie's need to make small talk with Noah on the drive. When she hung up, she was pleased to find Noah turning into the central precinct's parking garage.

Noah shifted into Park and met her gaze with a direct stare. "We'll have to walk a few blocks to get to the office. I really don't expect your assailant is stupid enough to attack you this close to the precinct, but stay close to me and keep alert. Just in case."

"Don't worry, I have no intention of wandering off." They got out of the vehicle and she was grateful when he didn't try to touch her.

They made their way up the ramp from the secured lower level assigned to police vehicles.

At street level, Noah held up his hand. "Wait here while I do a quick sweep."

He stepped onto the sidewalk and closely inspected the area around the garage before signaling for her to join him. He gestured at the garage wall. "I'll take the curb side. You, the interior."

She moved to the wall and he took off at a quick clip. She matched him stride for stride. Automobile and foot traffic were both heavy with workers trying to get to work on time. They had to wait at the stop light at the corner, and she felt vulnerable standing out in the open. She took a step closer to Noah before realizing what she'd done. He glanced at her, his surprise at her action written in his expression. She opened her mouth to make a smart-aleck comment to deflect the moment, but the light changed and they hurried across the street and down the sidewalk.

At the next corner, Noah held up his hand. "We'll turn right here. Let me check it out first."

He ran his gaze over the street, his focus intense. This was the Noah she'd seen at standoffs. Tough. Rock-solid and determined to resolve a situation without the loss of life.

"Okay, we're clear." He stepped aside, allowing her to join him.

Another hundred feet to go. Noah must be right. Her attacker was never going to show up there. With each step closer to their destination, relief hovered on the edge of her emotions, waiting to release fully once they were safely inside the precinct's secured inner door.

"Gun!" Noah suddenly shouted and his powerful arms came around her and hurled her to the ground.

SIX

Noah landed on his shoulder, the smell of damp concrete coming up to meet him. He made sure he took the brunt of the fall while cradling Darcie securely in his arms. *Pain* razored through his body, but he held fast to Darcie.

Bullets slammed into the wall above them. Fast. Fierce. To a layperson, it probably sounded like a submachine gun's staccatoed bursts, but Noah recognized it as a semiautomatic fired rapidly. He covered Darcie fully and held her in place. He hated putting his back to the shooters—it made him vulnerable—but there was no way he'd let a bullet touch her without going through him first.

"You okay?" he asked, glad that oxygen had found its way back into his lungs.

"Okay?" Her voice rose. "Okay? Someone is shooting at us. No, I'm not okay."

"I meant did I injure you on the takedown?"

"Oh, that. I might have scraped my knee. Again." She shifted, trying to get up.

He tightened his arms. "Stay down until I'm sure it's clear. They won't hang around for long."

"If I agree to stay plastered to the sidewalk will you loosen your grip?"

He relaxed his arms a fraction, but didn't leave even a finger's width between them.

He wished he could get up or at least lift his head to assess the situation. To check for pedestrians caught in the crossfire. But bullets continued to pelt the wall, raining shards of brick down on them. Another bullet pinged off a parking meter and embedded in the concrete just shy of his head.

He pressed Darcie harder to the ground and curled his body around her. Regret over pushing her face into the concrete had him back off a bit. She didn't speak, but he knew it had to be uncomfortable. Physically and mentally.

The gunfire finally stopped and tires screeched on the street. The smell of burning rubber and fumes from oil burning on the engine filled the air.

"They're taking off," he said.

She tried to squirm out from under him.

"Not yet," he warned and kept her in place. "We'll wait for officers to come out and clear the area."

"Isn't that overkill?" she asked, her voice muffled by police sirens winding up.

"Nothing is overkill when it comes to making sure you aren't harmed." The words came out with more force than he'd intended, catching him by surprise.

"I know you're uncomfortable," he said quickly to hide his heightened emotions. "But I wouldn't put you through this if I didn't think it absolutely necessary."

She didn't respond. They lay there, Noah's adrenaline ebbing and his awareness of her as a woman growing. Her unique scent. The way she felt in his arms. Much like he'd imagined many times before his past mistakes came to mind and popped the bubble. They could never be together. Not a woman who lost a child and a man who gave one away. The worst combination possible, in his mind.

"Lockhart," an officer called out from the precinct door. "Shooters have taken off. Patrol is on their tail. Hang tight while we clear the area."

Noah rolled away and Darcie shifted to face him. He glanced up and down the street for the first time since they'd hit the ground. Several officers were helping pedestrians, but Noah didn't see anyone who'd sustained injuries.

Please, God, let that be true.

He sat up and so did Darcie. She ran her fingers over the wall, slowing at the scars left by the bullets. He spotted a slug on the ground and picked it up. Great. A full metal jacketed 9 mm. Common ammo that wouldn't lead to their shooter. Still, the bullet didn't rule out a gangster. They often owned Tec 9 semiautomatic rifles because they were cheap. Add a thirty-round magazine and the gun could fire rapidly.

Darcie started twisting Haley's ring around her finger—faster and faster—then looked up. "You saved my life again. I can never repay you."

"It's my job."

She frowned and he wondered how his comment could possibly have upset her.

"What's with law enforcement officers?" she asked. "You do something heroic and then say it's your job? I hear that all the time with the FRS."

"Well, it *is* my job." Uncomfortable under her intense study, he looked at the shards of brick on the concrete.

"Yes, but you put your life on the line every day and yet you're all so humble about it. We need to celebrate the work police officers do and you all need to let us."

He looked back at her and held her gaze, trying to transmit how flawed he really was. "I'm not a hero, Darcie. Not some perfect guy you dreamed up. Far from it. I'm just an ordinary guy with a job to do."

"Right now, you're my hero." She leaned forward, took his hand and held it. "And you're not going to take that away from me. After everything I've been through in my personal life and with the job I do, I need to believe there is good in this world."

He stared at their hands and couldn't help but notice how well they fit together. "You don't need to go far to find goodness. You see it in your team all the time."

"I do, but I guess I take it for granted because I'm close to them. You, on the other hand, are not on the team and it's becoming quite clear that you're a good man."

He hoped so, but he doubted she'd continue to feel that way if she looked at his past. "Again, nothing unusual. There are a lot of good men in this world."

"Are there?" Her eyes narrowed.

He watched her for a moment and she dropped his hand, then squirmed under his gaze. "This is about Tom, isn't it?"

She shrugged.

"You don't want to talk about him," Noah said. "Is that just with me or with anyone?"

"Anyone," she whispered.

"Why?"

"There's no point in bringing up the past. It's done and over with."

"If it's as done as you say, shouldn't you be able to talk about it?"

"You don't understand—can't ever understand—what it's like to lose a child."

"Not to death, no, but..."

"But what?"

He looked away to stem any additional questions. He couldn't tell her about Evan. Not when she'd had her child taken away from her while he hadn't even been willing to see Ashley through her pregnancy. Sure, he wanted to make amends now, but according to Evan's adoptive parents, it was too late.

"So you don't want to talk, either," she said, sounding as sad as he felt inside.

Not with her. No. He'd tried that once with a serious girlfriend years before. She said she didn't even know him anymore. Didn't understand him or the way he'd bailed on Ashley. So how could a woman like Darcie, whose husband had walked out on her as he'd walked out on Ashley, who'd lost a child, understand it? She couldn't—so there was no point in telling her. He couldn't bear to see the loathing on her face.

"Guess that means you're not over whatever

it is, either," she said, parroting his words back at him.

"We're clear, Detective," the patrol officer announced.

Noah wasted no time and came to his feet. There was no longer a sense of urgency to get Darcie inside, but he wanted the conversation to end. He knew full well what he was doing. He was running away from the discussion. From her.

Hypocrite, asking her to spill her guts and you won't say a word.

Yeah, he was a hypocrite all right and despite the fact that the distasteful label ate at him, he'd continue to keep Evan a secret.

Noah put an arm around her shoulders and whisked her past the officers guarding the door and up to the second floor. At his cubicle, he helped her into a chair by his desk.

"Let me look at your knee." He squatted in front of her before she could argue.

"It's just a scratch."

He caught a good look at her torn khakis soaked with blood. "That's a lot of blood for just a scratch."

She shooed him out of the way and put her finger in the hole. She widened the opening and probed. Her no-nonsense approach to an injury that had to be stinging made Noah squeamish.

"Superficial cut," she announced. "I'm sure you have a first-aid kit, right?"

Noah nodded. "Otherwise, how are you? Any other injuries?"

"A few bumps, but I'm okay—thanks to you."

He studied her. "You'd tell me if you were hurt, right? I mean it's not one of those things you want to keep hidden."

She frowned at him.

"I'm sorry. I don't mean to keep harping on that."

"Then why do you?"

Yeah, why did he? Maybe because he wanted to get to know her better. But how did he get to know a woman who wouldn't talk about the very things that made her who she was?

It wasn't easy.

"So you don't need medical attention, then?"

"Nothing I can't handle with that first-aid kit."

"Right...I'll go see if there's any news on the shooter and have a clerk bring the first-aid kit to you."

"Sounds good," she said, her attention back on her knee.

He crossed the bullpen and asked a clerk to get the kit. He then stopped at Detective Bill Richter's desk, littered with candy wrappers, file folders and empty drink cups. Bill wore a rumpled shirt and creased pants. His shoes were scuffed and his hair too long. In a word, Bill was a mess to look at, but he was also a top-notch detective.

"What's the status on the shooter?" Noah cleared a corner of the desk and perched on it.

"Uniforms parked near the building pursued the car." Bill paused and scratched his chin. "Unfortunately, they lost them in the traffic."

"Seriously?" The word exploded from Noah's mouth, drawing the attention of his fellow officers. He lowered his voice. "We have how many uniforms out front and they can't tail a couple of gangsters?"

Bill eyed him.

"Okay, fine," Noah said. "It could happen to any of us. I'm just frustrated. Anyone get the plate?"

"Weren't any plates. Car was a late '90s Honda Accord. Too common to trace. Two males in the vehicle. Both Latino."

"I can't seem to catch a break," Noah muttered.

"Suppose you tell me what this is about and maybe I can help."

Noah filled him in on Darcie's attack the previous day.

"What about suspects?" Bill asked.

Noah listed them. "Actually, would you mind running a background check on Darcie and her ex for me?"

One of Bill's bushy eyebrows went up in a rainbow-sized arc. "Some reason you can't do that yourself?"

"Here's the thing." Noah bent closer as he tried to figure out how to tell Bill that he had thing for Darcie without coming right out and telling him he had thing for her. "I've known Darcie for quite a while. Her marriage didn't end well. I'm not sure I can be impartial when it comes to Tom."

Bill gave him an appraising look that every good detective could muster at a moment's notice. Noah didn't waver under the intense scrutiny.

"You'll owe me," he finally said.

Noah stifled a relieved sigh. "That I will."

"And you know I'll collect on it?"

"That I do."

"Then give me their particulars, and I'll check them out later today."

"I'll email it to you," Noah said. "But I need you to be thorough."

Bill rolled his eyes. "You'll get a thorough report, as usual."

Noah thanked Bill, then crossed the busy bullpen to his desk.

Darcie had finished bandaging her knee and was just disconnecting a phone call.

She shoved the phone into her pocket. "I knew our office would be talking about the shooting and I wanted Jake to know we're okay." She nodded at the far side of the room. "Was that conversation about the case?"

"Yes," he said, but wasn't about to share his discussion with Bill.

"They get the shooter?"

"No," he said, and before she could ask additional questions, he turned to his in-box to retrieve reports delivered by the clerk last night. "You still up for reviewing the callout list?"

"You'd better believe I am. No one shoots at us and gets away with it."

"That's my girl," he said, earning a raised eyebrow that he chose to ignore. He slid the report across his desk. "Detective Lewis is on vacation this week. I'll set you up at his desk."

She picked up the stack of papers and he led the way across the bullpen. He heard her limping behind him and each step made him madder. He'd promised to protect her and he'd nearly failed. Today had been a skinned knee. What might tomorrow bring? Or this afternoon? The next five minutes even.

He couldn't let his guard down for a moment. If he did, the consequences could be deadly.

Darcie pretended to look at the long list of her callouts, but she couldn't focus after the shooting. If not for Noah, she'd be dead. Dead! She'd put on a brave front for him, hiding the fear that had seemed to paralyze her as he'd protected her with his own body.

Her hero. No doubt about it. She'd almost said he was her knight in shining armor, but a knight's armor could tarnish while an act of heroism never went away. Tom had once been her knight, and look what had happened with him. Choosing to run when things got tough. When she needed him. Leaving her alone to battle her grief. To live the empty days filled with loss. With loneliness. With Haley's deserted room, her toys scattered on the floor as she'd left them. Elle, her big stuffed elephant sitting on the bed waiting for Haley to come home and snuggle every night.

Darcie had poured so many tears into Elle's fuzzy body while waiting for Tom to come to his senses. To man up and come home. But he didn't. Not even a phone call.

Pain pierced her heart, the ache feeling fresh and new, and coming from where, she didn't know. Tears welled up and she closed her eyes to keep them from falling.

She thought she'd made peace with her loss, but maybe she hadn't. Or maybe seeing Noah and the opportunity he represented for a fresh start, for a new relationship, brought it all back.

A reminder of what she could never have. Didn't want, right?

Right. She couldn't stand the pain of loss again. Couldn't survive it.

Argh. She was getting nowhere by letting her mind wander.

She grabbed the list and started down the first page. A few of the high-pressure responses were easy to recall, but the uneventful ones faded into each other. She checked off the ones she remembered. After she finished reviewing the entire report, if she hadn't found a lead, she would come back to the minor incidents to see if they held a clue.

She flipped the paper. Ran a finger down it. Check. Check. Check. Down the page she went. Nothing jumped out at her. She moved on to page three. Checked off the first six entries, then her pen paused over number seven.

Oleda Alverez. That had been a hairy response. A drug house. Open to the elements. Squatters inside. Filth. Garbage. Needles.

"Any success?" Noah asked from behind.

She tapped her pen on Oleda's name. "This one was interesting."

"A woman? Not something I expected." He sat on the desk, closer than she would like.

She eased her chair back to create some distance, which earned her a raised eyebrow. She didn't care. She had to do everything necessary to protect her heart.

"Oleda wasn't the problem," she explained. "In fact, she was the victim. It was her boyfriend who unloaded on me."

Noah flexed his jaw. "Tell me about him."

"We arrived on scene. Drug house. Oleda had been shot. Everyone was too high to tell us what had happened. So we treated and transported her to the hospital. There was really no point. We knew she was in bad shape when we arrived on scene and she had a slim chance of making it. Still, you have to hope, right? Do your best and make the transport. But she died in the rig."

"So you got her to the hospital?"

Darcie nodded. "That's where the boyfriend lost it. Doctors met us at the rig where they pronounced Oleda. The boyfriend had followed the ambulance. He came running over and went ballistic. Blamed me. Said if I had done a better job, gotten there sooner and so on, that she'd be fine. He called me every name in the book. Even threatened to get even with me."

"You catch his name?"

"No, but now I wish I had."

"Can you describe him?"

She searched her memory, ticking through the events until she could call him up. "He was Latino. Stocky. Maybe five-ten, two hundred twenty pounds. He was wearing a blue-and-white shirt."

"Like your attacker?" Noah asked.

"Yeah. Similar, I think." The hospital scene played in living color in her brain. "The guy at the hospital had a symbol on his sleeve. An N with a—" Realization sent her gaze flying to Noah. "My attacker... His shirt. It had the symbol on it, too. It was a large number fourteen with the letter N at the bottom of the four."

"Nuevo gang insignia."

"That's the gang you suspected my attacker belongs to, isn't it?"

"Yes. And the boyfriend you described was of the same build and size as your attacker, too."

"Wait, you think... Couldn't be. Right? Oleda's boyfriend and my attacker are one in the same?"

"You're the one who needs to answer that question. Could this guy be your attacker?"

Darcie searched deep in her memory. "I can't come up with a clear face for Oleda's boyfriend. But when I saw my attacker yesterday, I didn't recognize him. I think he'd at least look familiar if he was Oleda's boyfriend."

Noah sat staring ahead for a few moments, looking like he was processing the information. "Let's review what we know. The gang symbol suggests Oleda's boyfriend is in the same gang as your attacker. Is there anything about the boy-friend that you can think of to absolutely rule him out as your attacker?"

She ran the night like a video through her mind. "No."

"Then we need to locate this guy."

"But how?"

"We'll start with Oleda's homicide investigation. Since my team didn't handle the case it had to have happened outside the city limits."

"Right." She described a neighborhood on Portland's east side.

"Means Oleda's homicide investigation would have been done by County. Or if the shooting was gang-related, then the gang task force would have handled it." He stood, that resolved look of determination on his face again. "I'll call Skyler after lunch to see who ran the investigation and try to get a copy of the file."

"Lunch? Really? There's no way I can eat a thing."

"You have to keep your strength up." He seemed to want to say something else but clamped down on his lips.

It didn't matter. His expression said it all. She needed her strength to stay a step ahead of a dangerous killer. One who appeared to have gang affiliations. One who possessed powerful weapons. And one who wasn't afraid to try to kill with a whole precinct of police officers standing at the ready.

SEVEN

"I wish you'd reconsider and take me with you," Darcie said as she stepped past Noah and into the firehouse. "I might see something in Oleda's neighborhood that you'd miss."

Noah ground his teeth to keep from snapping at her. They'd been over and over this on the drive to the firehouse. There was no way he'd allow her to accompany him to the run-down neighborhood where Oleda had lived.

"I'm not changing my mind." Noah clicked the dead bolt into place behind her. She was in danger, serious danger, and even if she wasn't, he certainly wouldn't take her to another gang-infested neighborhood.

He took a moment to let his gaze run over every inch of the place in view. He was on edge and attuned to every sound and movement. Had been from the moment he'd escorted her out of the precinct through their sally port—a secure, controlled entryway used to process criminals.

He only wished he'd realized how desperate her attacker was before the shooting this morning. He could have used the sally port then, too. He'd considered it, but he hadn't wanted to parade her past holding cells and subject her to prisoner catcalls.

He trailed her into the family room, listening beyond the sharp staccato of her heels ringing from the concrete floors to the high ceiling. Beyond the large metal air ducts clicking and groaning above as the heat turned off. Straining to hear anything out of the ordinary. Anything signaling danger. She settled on the sofa. He took a seat next to her and could feel her unease. He wished he could do something to make it better.

He'd tried to make her as comfortable as possible at the precinct, and he'd called off going to the firing range to assess her skills. She didn't need to be around the sound of gunfire today. Plus, he'd do his best to be with her 24/7 and if not, he'd be sure one of her teammates stood guard until this was resolved, so he needn't worry about how well she could handle her gun. That could wait until after they apprehended her attacker.

After. Right. He wouldn't be part of her life then. They'd be back to the dance of avoidance and she'd never go to the range with him. The thought brought an ache to his gut.

She reached for a pillow. The scarf around her neck fell open to reveal a circle of angry green-and-purple bruises. He'd caught a glimpse of them before, but hadn't seen the extent of the damage.

Visions of this creep's fingers clamped around her delicate skin came to mind. Anger roared through him. This was precisely why he wouldn't take her to Oleda's place. In fact, he shouldn't go, either. He should stay right here with Darcie and send another detective to do the interview. Someone else could question the neighbors, but no one else could ensure her safety as well as he could.

She started to adjust the scarf.

"Why didn't you tell me it was this bad?" He reached out to touch her neck.

She jerked back, putting distance between them. "Because I didn't want to see that look on your face."

"What look?" He lowered his hand, as his touch was clearly unwelcome.

"Pity. Sadness. Desire to run the other way."

"You're reading an awful lot into one look, don't you think?"

"Trust me. Plenty of people gave me the exact same look after Haley died, and I've had enough of it to last a lifetime." She sighed.

"I'm sure they were only trying to show you they cared and were worried for you."

"True. They did. And at first, I appreciated it. But after time passed and I started to come out of the depths of my grief, I realized the Darcie I'd once been with my friends had ceased to exist. I had become the Darcie who lost her child. The woman no one knew what to say to. The woman to hold at a distance or completely avoid because that was the easiest thing to do."

He started to reach for her hand, but at her terse look, he stopped. "I'm sorry you had to go through that."

"See?" She gestured at his face. "There it is again. I don't want 'sorry.' I don't want pity. I want to be seen for who I am. I've come to realize that grief changes form, but it will never end. Haley will always be in my heart. I'll always long to hold her again. To talk to her. But I recognized back then that I had to move on or I'd drive myself crazy. I couldn't let Haley's loss be the only thing that defined me. The same thing is true of this attack. I can't just be a victim. I have to move on. Your pity doesn't help. It makes me want to sink into despair, but I won't let it take over." She crossed her arms and glared at him.

She was stronger than he'd thought, but no matter what she claimed, she hadn't really moved on from Haley's death. If she had, she wouldn't be so against dating. Against having children again. A stance she'd made clear over the last six years. And she was also wrong about him.

"Know this, Darcie," he said earnestly. "I don't pity you. I don't feel sorry for you. I admire your strength, and if you're seeing anything in my look, it's that I feel bad for not being there when you needed a friend. For failing you."

Her eyes widened. "You're not my protector. I can take care of myself."

"I'm everyone's protector," he said before thinking it through. He, like most police officers, felt a heavy burden to help others. Not just on duty, but all the time. That's why most officers carried a gun even when they were off duty. He couldn't fathom being in a situation where he couldn't take action to save a life or intervene when a criminal took advantage of the innocent.

She smiled but it was forced. "I get that you're on guard all the time. I know that sense of responsibility from my teammates, and, in a way, I do the same thing with medical issues. But make no mistake, Noah. I am capable. I can take care of myself."

"Like when you readily drew your weapon?"

"Okay, fine." She jutted out her chin. "You had to force me to pull out my gun. But who's to say if I hadn't called you, I wouldn't have taken it out on my own?"

"Ah, see, there's the thing. You *did* call me. First. Before doing anything else. You wanted help because you knew your skills were limited. That's the smart thing to do—recognize when a situation is something you're not equipped to handle and call someone with the training to step in. So stop fighting my help and concern for your well-being. Accept it for what it is. It doesn't make you weak or less of a person. It doesn't make you Pitiful Darcie. It makes you Smart Darcie. A woman who knows her limitations and accepts help when needed."

"Fine." She relaxed her arms and her shoulders slumped.

"And don't feel defeated. There is no one on this earth who doesn't need help at some time."

"Even you?"

"Well, maybe not me." He grinned to show her he was kidding. "Can we reach an agreement that you'll stop thinking I pity you and accept my help going forward?"

"Yes," she said, albeit reluctantly. "But only your *help*. Nothing more. This thing—" she gestured between them "—this attraction or whatever you want to a call it, goes no further."

He started to tell her he didn't intend to take it any further when Archer walked into the room. His gaze went from Noah to Darcie and back again. "Looks like I'm interrupting something serious."

"No," they said in unison.

"Right." Archer leaned against the wall, watching them.

Noah had always respected Archer, but had also felt uneasy around him. The guy was so in tune with things it was like he could read your mind. Something Noah didn't need in his life.

"Everything okay with Isabel and Pilar?" Darcie asked.

"They're both fine. Isabel is napping and I suspect Pilar's taking the time to do the same thing." Archer turned his focus to Noah. "Would now be a good time to bring you up to speed on what I've found on Kerr Development?"

Noah gestured at a club chair. "Take a seat and fill us in."

Archer sat on the edge of the chair and planted his arms on his knees. He leaned forward, looking intense and businesslike.

"First, let me tell you that Kerr Development is a privately held business," Archer said. "This means they don't have to publish the same reports as a public company, giving me limited access to their finances. But I *was* able to learn that a good deal of their income is generated from retail rentals in the many malls they own across the metro area."

"I had no idea they owned malls," Noah said.

Archer nodded. "They have more retail space than any other single company in the city and they report having the lowest vacancy rate, as well."

"So they're doing okay financially?" Noah asked.

"That's what it looks like on the surface, but here's the odd thing," Archer said, warming to his subject. "I decided to check out some of the malls reporting one-hundred-percent occupancy and I found quite a few vacant storefronts."

"I don't understand," Darcie said. "They say it's full, but it's not? Why do that?"

"Only reason that makes sense to me is that they want someone to think they're doing better than they actually are."

"Someone, like who?" Noah asked.

"Potential investors. Builders looking to develop malls. Their board of directors or even Winnie, if she's not active in the day-to-day operations and relies on reports." Archer leaned closer. "But that's not the oddest part. I called the phone numbers posted on the vacant storefronts and was told they're rented."

"Maybe someone just rented them," Darcie offered.

"I'd think that, too, except I asked about spaces all around town. I even had other team members call in case they recognized my voice. We were all told there were no vacancies."

"So let me get this straight," Noah said. "They have empty retail space, but when potential renters call, they turn them away."

Archer nodded. "Makes no sense. With retail rents the way they are, they've got to be losing money on these properties, and yet, it doesn't seem as if they are."

"Weird," Noah said. "Can you dig deeper?"

"I've got a few contacts I can check with."

"I appreciate it, man." Noah looked at Darcie, who seemed as puzzled as they all were. "We can ask Winnie about this when we meet with her."

Darcie frowned. "She's not very involved with the business anymore, but hopefully she can shed some light on it."

Noah could see she was hesitant about approaching Winnie. The team owed Winnie a lot and probably felt a little ungrateful to Darcie to repay the woman by digging into her business affairs. He wished he didn't have to question her, either. He'd be diplomatic with the older woman, but he had to ask tough questions.

"How's the rest of the investigation going?" Archer asked.

Noah brought Archer up to speed and an idea hit him. "I was just about to go over to Oleda's former address to see what I can find out about her boyfriend. Since you're not working today, would you be willing to go instead?"

"Be happy to help in any way I can." Archer pushed to his feet.

"Wait." Darcie shot Noah a look. "You're passing this off? Shouldn't you be the one to do the questioning?"

"Don't trust me, huh, Darcie?" Archer joked.

"It's not that, I—"

"I don't know of any police officer who is better tuned in to people and their nuances than Archer," Noah interrupted. "If there's something to be gained from this visit, he'll find it, even if it's something no one's willing to say out loud."

"I know, but…" She shrugged.

"But you think I'm shirking my duty."

"No. I don't know…maybe. We have to find this guy. And soon. Before he strikes again."

"Trust me," Noah said, making strong eye contact with her. "I know exactly what this guy is capable of and that's why I'm not letting you out of my sight."

Darcie grabbed her knitting and shifted on the overstuffed chair in the game room. She had to do something to keep her nerves at bay and keep her mind off Noah as he watched her like a hawk. He was in Jake's favorite chair at a round table across the room, working on a puzzle of one of Portland's twelve bridges. Jake always had a jigsaw puzzle in progress. He claimed it helped clear his mind, but she didn't get it. That many pieces needing sorting and combing through drove her crazy. Now knitting was another story. Making scarves, mittens and hats for foster children usually relaxed her.

Not today, though. Not stuck in this room with Noah, each of them engrossed in their own thoughts. As much as she willed her mind not to, it kept rewinding to the morning attack and Noah's care. To the way he'd put his life on the line for her. Shielded her from bullets with his body. He'd been her hero and the thought of a man with hero potential who went beyond friendship in her life thrilled her as much as it scared her.

She sighed.

Noah looked up. Their eyes met. A strange catch settled in her chest and she jerked her focus back to her knitting. There was something more developing between them despite their best efforts to fight it. Despite her not having a clue what he was thinking. What he seemed to want to tell her but kept backing off from revealing.

Perhaps he was just like Tom. A man who internalized his emotions until one day he lost control and disappeared. Perhaps all men were like that.

Okay, fine, she knew better than that. She worked with strong, compassionate men who, though they didn't talk about their feelings, stuck around through the hard stuff.

So she was willing to concede that there were men out there she could trust. Signs had always pointed to Noah being one of those men, but now? Now she wasn't sure. She liked knowing he was physically there to protect her. Liked being in his company. Liked *him,* for that matter.

"Hey," Archer said from the doorway.

"You're back." She dropped the knitting to her lap and waited for him to share news about his visit.

Noah crossed the room. "Tell me you found something for us to go on."

"Wish I did." Archer stepped closer, his eyebrows drawn in a scowl, making Darcie cringe inside. "I talked to quite a few people but everyone clammed up as soon as I mentioned Oleda. You know how close-knit Latino communities can be. Especially when law enforcement starts asking questions."

Darcie had experienced the same thing on callouts. It was incredibly frustrating when people refused to give her details about an illness or injury because they didn't want to reveal anything that might draw police attention to them, but she still understood it. "Many of them came from a country where they really can't trust law enforcement or elected officials, so I don't blame them one bit."

"True," Noah said. "They have a reason, all right. But if that doesn't change, we're never going to get a handle on gangs."

"On the bright side," Archer said, "my visit wasn't a total bust. I noticed Oleda's brother was sporting a Nuevo gang tattoo on his hand."

"Nuevo. We expected the gang connection, but it's still hard to hear." Darcie felt the fear from her attack returning but she wouldn't let it get to her. She had to be proactive now. She turned to Noah. "How does this new lead move us forward?"

"It doesn't. At least not without additional information." He dug out his phone. "It's time for me to follow up with Detective Judson again. He's the detective who handled Oleda's case. I need to find out why he's not returning my call." Dialing his phone, Noah stepped into the hallway.

Darcie watched him go, her thoughts returning to the fact that he'd given the interview task to Archer. If Noah had done the interviews, might he have come up with more information? Archer was intuitive, as Noah had said, and Darcie respected his skills, but he wasn't an experienced detective like Noah.

Archer dropped into the chair next to her

and watched her carefully. "Something bothering you?"

Should she confide in him? As a negotiator, he was an excellent listener and he never gossiped. He could be trusted to keep everything she said private. And it would be good to talk to someone about Noah.

"I don't mean to pry," Archer went on. "Just thought you might want to talk about whatever has you looking so upset."

"It's Noah," she said quickly before she changed her mind. "I'm getting mixed signals from him. One minute it seems like the investigation is his top priority. The next he's laid-back about it."

"So?"

"So either he's committed to the investigation or he's not."

Archer stared at her with an unflinching gaze. "He's committed, all right. You're just not ready to see how committed he might be."

"What's that supposed to mean?"

"Nothing." He shook his head.

"No, seriously. What are you not saying?"

He took a deep breath and his expression turned serious. "Maybe it's time you let go of your past and take an honest look at the people in your life. You might be surprised by what you find."

"Like what?"

"Like you have a whole team who not only

support you professionally, but would do the same thing in your personal life if you'd give us a chance." He searched her face for a moment and came away looking sad. "But that would mean confiding in us, and I know that's not something you're willing to do."

She'd opened the door to this conversation and now she wished she hadn't. "You say that like it's wrong to want to keep my private life private."

"Wrong? No. Hard for you? Yes."

"I can't help it." The minute the words came out she knew it wasn't true. She was choosing not to let anyone in. Something she wasn't ready to change.

Fortunately, Archer didn't call her on it, and she sat back with a sigh.

"Anything else I can do to help with the investigation?" he asked.

Was there? She was so used to doing things on her own that she was rusty at asking for favors. But Archer wanted to lend a hand and she did have one thing she'd been thinking about. "Since you profile criminals, you could give me your take on the creep who attacked me."

Archer pondered her request for a moment. "Wish I could help with that, but I don't have enough to go on."

"What about the fact that it's seeming like he's a gang member?"

"Well…" Archer lifted his face in thought. "Assuming we're correct in his gang affiliation—which we have no concrete evidence of, at this point—it would be unusual for a gangster to try to strangle you. They're more apt to shoot you right off the bat."

"Wow, thanks."

"Hey." He laughed. "I didn't mean you, per se. I meant when a typical gangster takes a life it's often an emotionally driven decision to retaliate against a perceived insult from another gang, and he'd use whatever was at hand to get the job done. Which usually means guns and knives. Or he'd even run you down with his car."

Darcie frowned. "Why the strangling then?"

"I'd have to say it's extremely personal. Maybe to him or to the gang. Someone who thinks you've wronged him in some way, has a vendetta against you, and wants to see you die right before his eyes."

His ominous tone sent a shiver running through her. "I don't even know any gangsters much less harmed one of them."

"Except the perceived harm to Oleda."

"Right, except that."

Archer stared ahead, perhaps watching Noah pass by the doorway as he paced up and down the hallway, his phone to his ear. "You sure Noah's on the right track and your attack wasn't random? Maybe an attempted rape?"

Darcie had asked to keep the hit list on a need-to-know basis and until now, Archer hadn't needed to know so she shared it with him. She glanced at the doorway and waited for Noah to move past the opening. When he did, she removed the scarf from around her neck. "Besides. Does this look like he wanted to sexually assault me or kill me?"

"Man, Darcie, I'm sorry. He really did a number on you." Archer's gaze held concern, but not the pity she endured after Haley died.

"I think it would be helpful if you talked to someone about this," he continued.

"I am talking to someone. You."

"I mean a professional who's trained to deal with trauma."

She forced a laugh. "That's your go-to, isn't it? Suggesting a shrink for every problem."

"Counseling got me through some rough times in my life and made me believe in its effectiveness."

"Would you like to talk about it?" she asked, mimicking his soothing tone.

"Ha!" He shook his head and grinned. "Nice try, kiddo. Nice try. Maybe when you open up about your past, I'll tell you about mine."

She shrugged.

"Right. Just as I suspected." He got up and stared down at her, his gaze probing, encouraging her to speak.

She'd never felt the urge to tell anyone about Tom or Haley because she didn't want their pity. But after seeing Archer's response a moment ago, maybe she could share a bit more with her teammates. Be less guarded. Perhaps.

"So hold it in, but don't be surprised if it all blows up in your face." After another long look, he left the room, leaving Darcie alone in her confusion.

Noah suddenly stopped moving near the doorway, drawing her attention. His face was familiar. Like an old friend. His jaw slightly crooked. A light wave to his hair. Eyes that held secrets, if his earlier comment about losing a child was to be believed. She had a sudden desire to unearth those secrets he'd hinted at. To find out what he was keeping from her.

A desire that turned to unease when he stowed his phone and stepped into the room. His gaze sought her out. The urge to ask about his past was so strong she was already forming the question in her mind.

Could she talk to Noah without losing it? Maybe be less guarded in general, not only with the team, but with Noah, too?

If she took that step, what would happen then?

EIGHT

Two hours later, the front door opened and Noah shot to his feet, his hand automatically going to his gun.

"Relax," Darcie said from her seat in the corner of the game room. "It's most likely Skyler."

He wasn't about to relax until he confirmed with his own two eyes that it was indeed Skyler. He moved to the hallway, ready to act. Skyler rounded the corner and he blew out a breath before she or Darcie saw how much of himself he'd invested in protecting Darcie. How much the mere thought of an intruder made him as jumpy as a kangaroo.

He looked at Skyler's hands, hoping to see the file on Oleda's murder investigation. When he'd called Skyler after lunch, she'd told him that the metro gang task force had taken charge of Oleda's case. She'd offered to call Judson to obtain a copy, and Noah had agreed, as he'd hoped she'd have more luck in getting through to Judson.

"Still no file on Oleda, I see," he said.

"I left a message with Judson."

"Let me guess. No response yet."

She nodded briskly.

"Well, at least I now know the guy isn't just blowing me off," Noah said.

"I've worked with Judson several times and he's not one to ignore phone calls without good reason," she pointed out. "Whatever's going down with his team has to be big."

Noah had thought the same thing, but he hadn't let his thoughts end there. "I can't help but wonder if it somehow ties to our investigation."

"All we can do is wait until we hear from him."

Something Noah didn't want to do.

"Where's Darcie?" Skyler asked.

"Game room."

After another short nod, she stepped down the hallway with purpose, like she had something important to tell her friend.

Noah followed her into the room, apprehension tightening his gut. Not that his gut had relaxed much since this whole thing started with Darcie. He couldn't remember a time in his life that he'd been so uneasy.

Skyler crossed the room to Darcie. "I thought Noah looked rough, but you look—"

Darcie flipped up a hand. "No need to tell me.

I know I'm a mess, but I guess someone shooting at me qualifies as a bad day." She winked like this was all a big joke.

Noah appreciated that she could joke, but he didn't find anything funny about her comment.

"Not sure this will help, but I have some news." Skyler took out her small investigator's notebook.

"Let's have it," Noah snapped, but when both heads shot up to look at him, he faked a smile. "Sorry. I'm getting tired of hitting brick walls. Go ahead."

Skyler sat in a leather club chair. "I've ruled out two of the three Leland Kings, but the third one raises all kinds of red flags." She met Noah's gaze directly, and that sick feeling in his gut intensified. "He lives in Eugene and was reported missing by his sister four days ago. Uniforms did a welfare check. He wasn't home, but they found blood on his sofa. No other sign of foul play."

"Missing. Maybe dead," Noah said.

"I didn't say that."

"You don't have to. He's missing. He has a slash through his name on the hit list. That says it all." Noah purposely avoided eye contact with Darcie, as he didn't want to see the added strain on her face. "Anything in his background check to link him to gang activity or Darcie's attack?"

Skyler shook her head. "He seems to be an upstanding citizen. No criminal record. Not even a speeding ticket. He's a graphic designer and owns his own firm. Late fifties. Never married. Nothing to suggest he was involved in anything nefarious."

Darcie sat forward. "Do they have any idea what happened to him?"

"None," Skyler answered. "The detective in charge of the case isn't sure if there was foul play or if Leland cut himself eating dinner in front of the TV, or something innocent like that. They checked area ERs and clinics. He didn't seek medical attention."

"I'll need to talk to the detective," Noah said.

"Way ahead of you." Skyler ripped a page from her notebook and handed it to him. "Here's his contact information. He's very interested in your hit list, and I told him you'd be calling."

Noah took the paper. "Strong detective work, Skyler. Thanks for your help."

"Glad to do it."

"I'll make an appointment to meet with him as soon as possible. I'll want to see King's home and review the detective's casebook."

"Casebook?" Darcie asked.

"An indexed file of everything from witness statements to medical reports and an evidence log," Noah replied. "A good detective will have a neat and organized file that I can copy."

Skyler closed her notebook. "I also ran a thorough check on Pilar. She's squeaky clean."

Darcie frowned. "I hate that you have to investigate them when they haven't done anything wrong."

"Can't be helped," Noah said. "They're a part of this through no fault of their own."

Darcie jutted out her chin, looking like an adorable, pouty child. "Then you should investigate me, too."

"Already am," Noah replied without a bit of hesitation. "Or at least one of my fellow detectives is running a check on you."

Her mouth dropped open.

"It's protocol, Darcie," Skyler added.

"I know, but—"

"But you're worried we might learn something about your past that you haven't volunteered," Skyler interrupted.

Darcie fiddled with her ball of yarn. "I don't have anything to hide, but yeah. My past is my story to tell. Not something I want you to learn from some report."

"There's a solution to that." Noah locked eyes with Darcie, waiting for her to capitulate and talk about her past.

She held his stare and returned it ounce for ounce. He felt the tension rolling off her, but she didn't bat an eye. Didn't say a word. *Fine.*

She still didn't plan on sharing her past with him. He deserved that. He hadn't told her about Evan, either.

"I'm still working on Mayte," Skyler went on as if he and Darcie weren't engaged in a stare down.

Noah changed his focus to Skyler. "I suspect she has a long arrest record."

Skyler nodded. "Which is why it's taking longer to pull together. I've requested case files for each of her arrests to see if any of them are gang-related."

"For Isabel's and Pilar's sake, I hope the answer is no," Darcie said with grim certainty.

Noah wasn't optimistic. He suspected Mayte's habitual drug use brought her in contact with gangs, and he wouldn't be surprised if they discovered a connection to Darcie's attack.

Darcie took a breath before answering Noah's request to spend the night at the firehouse to keep watch over her. He looked stubbornly set in his decision, but Darcie wasn't ready to concede yet. She couldn't. Just the thought of him staying close by all night sent unwanted emotions firing.

"Well?" he asked, looking hopeful.

"I'm not declining your help," she said as firmly as she could without making him think she was ungrateful. "But I'm well protected with the team surrounding me. You don't need to stay here tonight."

"I get that, I honestly do, but for my own peace of mind I have to be close by." He planted his hands on his waist and met her gaze. "If you say no, I'll sleep in the car."

"That's not the answer. You'll be uncomfortable and I'll feel guilty all night."

"Then the solution is to let me stay here."

She sighed and knew it was time to give in. "I'm already sleeping on the couch in my condo so Pilar and Isabel can share my bed. You'll have to make do down here." She nodded at the large sofa in the family room. "Is that close enough for you?"

"Sure. As long as you promise not to leave the property via the back door."

"I'm not going anywhere. I promise."

"We're ready, Darcie," Isabel called out from the down the hall in the game room.

Her sweet little voice sounding so eager and ready for a simple game of Go Fish lightened Darcie's mood and she vowed to forget the drama of her life to help provide Isabel with a tension-free atmosphere.

"Mind if I join you?" Noah asked.

"You seriously want to play Go Fish?"

"Are you kidding?" His lips tipped in a charming grin, sending her heart singing. "When I was growing up, I was the champion Go Fish player in all of Washington County."

"They had tournaments, did they?" Darcie said snidely as they headed for the game room.

"What?" He gave her a look of mock surprise. "You've never heard of them?"

"I grew up in Florida. Though I'm sure the tournament was a momentous occasion, your wins didn't make the national news."

He tossed back his head and laughed. The joyful sound melted her heart. Just like that. Into a puddle. She loved seeing this lighter side of him. It was something she desperately needed in her own life. She'd survived the loss of Haley, the abandonment of Tom, but joy? She could honestly say she hadn't found that again.

Lord, did You put Noah in my life to show me the way back?

It was thinking like this that was the very reason he shouldn't be staying the night. She needed to make sure they weren't ever alone together. She hurried ahead of him into the game room painted a cheerful yellow. Isabel and Pilar sat at a table in front of a wall of shelves filled with books and board games.

Pillar looked up. She looked weary and her shoulders sagged. Darcie stopped by the older woman and rested her hand on Pilar's forehead before taking her pulse.

Pilar forced a smile. "You do not need to fuss."

"Shh," Noah said. "If you argue, it'll just take longer, 'cause once she's made up her mind..." He winked.

Darcie looked up at him and couldn't help but smile. "You know me that well, do you, Noah Lockhart?"

His gaze darkened. "I guess as well as you'll let anyone know you, yes."

His serious response took her aback for a moment and she stared at him. She hadn't expected an honest answer when they'd been joking. She wasn't surprised that the good humor in the room had evaporated and tension took its place.

"Can we please start?" Isabel begged from her seat across the table.

Pilar cast a warning look at Isabel and shook her head.

Isabel's happy expression crumpled and Darcie's heart cracked. The child had been through so much. Pilar was trying to make up for it, but the years of neglect remained in Isabel's eyes at times. Darcie had cherished Haley. Tried to be the mother Darcie had never had growing up. And when Darcie saw another child suffering, she couldn't stand by and not get involved.

Darcie could best help Isabel by keeping the mood light around here and making sure Pilar fully recovered.

Darcie turned back to Pilar. "I can tell you're exhausted. You should go up to bed."

"But Isabel…"

"Go Fish can be played with three people." Noah stepped over to Pilar and helped her stand. "Darcie and I will take care of Isabel."

"Absolutely." Darcie ruffled Isabel's curls. "It's always a pleasure to spend time with this little munchkin."

Isabel looked up at Darcie. "What's a munchkin?"

"I'll explain as we play Go Fish." Darcie started to shuffle the cards and Noah escorted Pilar out of the room.

He cupped her good arm and moved slowly. Gently. Tenderly, as he'd done after Darcie's attack. Of course, she'd been too freaked out to appreciate how considerate he'd been. And then, she'd added to his challenge by trying to fight him. By continuing to fight him. He didn't deserve that. Plus her actions could be distracting when he needed to focus. She'd seen officers who'd let distractions get in the way—it often resulted in injury. One died of a gunshot to the chest. Right on her gurney.

She shuddered at the memory. She couldn't cause the same thing to happen to Noah.

"I can deal the cards if you can't," Isabel proclaimed.

Darcie slid the cards to the precious little girl and her thoughts turned to games played with Haley. To the crisp, cool day in the fall when Haley buried herself in a pile of colorful maple leaves at the curb. To the senior citizen who'd lost control of his car. Jumped the curb.

Darcie had seen it happen right in front of her eyes, as if in slow motion. She hadn't been able to stop the man from losing control of his car. She also couldn't control the chances of something bad happening to Noah as they searched for her attacker.

She had to face facts. No matter how hard she tried, she had no control over life-and-death matters. That would never change, and unless it did, her recent thoughts of opening up to others didn't matter one little bit.

NINE

Noah sat at the bar in the firehouse kitchen, his first morning cup of coffee on the countertop. He stretched and yawned. The sofa had been comfortable. The sheets soft. The blanket warm. But no amount of comfort was going to make him forget about the danger surrounding Darcie and drop off to a restful sleep. He'd nod off for a few hours, then jerk awake. Over and over again. So what if he was dragging this morning. A few cups of coffee and he'd be alert and ready.

But first a call to Judson. Noah hoped that he'd catch Judson before he started his day and the guy would actually pick up his phone.

The phone rang four times and just as Noah prepared himself to get Judson's voice mail, the detective answered. Noah stifled a hallelujah and identified himself.

"Yeah, right," Judson said. "You wanted information on the Nuevo gang. Sorry I didn't get back with you. Things have been crazy. In fact, I've only got a few minutes, so make this quick."

Noah explained Darcie's attack and Oleda's connection to Darcie. "We're looking for the boyfriend."

"I know the guy. Name's Elonzo Perez. He's a Nuevo, all right. His rap sheet is about a mile long. Violent dude. Can't tell you where to find him, though."

Noah grabbed a pen and jotted down the name. "And Oleda? I know as a woman she wouldn't have been allowed in the gang, but was her death connected to them?"

"Yeah. At least we suspect it was. She was killed in a drive-by meant to take down a rival gang member. To avoid prosecution on a drug charge, he'd cut a deal and snitched on the Nuevo leaders."

"Which wouldn't make him popular with the Nuevos or his own gang."

"No one abides a snitch."

The beep from a remote car entry filtered through the phone and it sounded like Judson was on the move.

"Was it a Nuevo or a member of the rival gang who took down the snitch?" Noah asked before Judson could end the call.

"We don't have enough evidence to point a finger at either one of them. Since a Nuevo would have backed off once he saw Oleda, seems likely the rival gang was taking out one of their own. They were at a local festival and Oleda just happened to be in the wrong place at the wrong time."

Noah thought back to all the briefings he'd attended on gangs and remembered something about family respect. "Gangs have that whole family thing going on, right?"

"Exactly. If a family member is present, all gang business ceases. Which on the one hand is odd, because in this case, the rival gang would have the same values and should have backed off when they saw Oleda. Plus you'd think they'd let the snitch live to testify and cripple the Nuevo gang before doing him in."

"Was the snitch's information damaging enough that the Nuevos would ignore their family rule?"

"Maybe. If the snitch hadn't died, his testimony would have put the Nuevo leaders away for a long time."

"Just exactly what did the snitch say?" Noah asked.

"Sorry, man. That information is on a need-to-know basis."

"Then you can tell me because I need to know."

"Nice try." Judson chuckled. "Look man, I gotta go."

"One more thing," Noah said, hoping to keep him on the line. "The Nuevo gang leaders. Did you have enough to arrest them without the testimony?"

"Unfortunately, no. We're hoping to get one of them to turn on the others, but we're still looking for them. They went underground when the snitch died."

"I don't get it. The snitch is dead. Why go underground?"

"Who knows what motivates them to do what they do?" Judson said, sounding disgusted. "But maybe they think we have another snitch."

"Could this be connected to the attack I'm investigating?"

Judson was silent for a moment. "Anything is possible."

Not a helpful or very comforting response. Noah needed more. "I need to get a look at the information your snitch provided."

"Sorry, man. Best I can do is ask my LT to let me read you in on the investigation."

Noah stifled a sigh of frustration. "Do that and let me know ASAP what you learn."

"Will do." Judson paused for a moment and didn't disconnect. "You know, it might not be a bad idea to leave your investigation alone for a while. The Nuevos are in turmoil and things are extremely volatile in their neighborhood. You don't want to get in the middle of that. And you don't want to mess with Perez. He's the kind of guy who wouldn't need much provocation to kill."

Noah wasn't about to be warned off if it meant finding the man who'd attacked Darcie. He thanked Judson for the information, then called dispatch to look up Elonzo Perez in the PPB's database and email his rap sheet. The minute his face flashed on Noah's phone, a long list of priors below, Noah knew this man was as dangerous as Judson had claimed.

Noah hated to think of showing the picture to Darcie, but if Perez had attacked her, she'd need to ID him. Noah found her still sitting on the patio, where he'd left her, a cup of coffee untouched on the table. He stepped outside. The sun spilled yellow rays over the garden, making all the colors richer—the warm chestnut of her hair, the coffee brown of her eyes, even the vibrant blue of her jacket. She peered up at him.

"What's wrong?" she asked, her breath rising in little puffs of cold air around her face.

"I talked to Judson. Oleda's boyfriend is Elonzo Perez." He handed over his phone. "Recognize him?"

She studied the picture and Noah expected she'd react, but she didn't move. She simply stared long and hard at the screen.

"Yeah," she finally said, almost dispassionately. "He's the guy who threatened me at the hospital."

"And is he your attacker?"

"Could be, but I'm not positive." She handed his phone back to him. "What happens now?"

"Now I get an arrest warrant and an alert issued for Perez and send someone by his last known address to serve the warrant."

"Do you think they'll find him at home?"

Noah thought back to his conversation with Judson. If Perez was caught up in the Nuevo turmoil, the odds of finding him at all were slim, but Darcie didn't need to know that.

"Could be. Why don't we let the police force concentrate on that while we head to Eugene to interview Detective Wilson about Leland King?"

She nodded, but it was halfhearted. "In other words, Perez will be hard to find."

"You can read my mind now, huh?" He chuckled.

She didn't respond. Something was troubling her this morning and, as usual, she didn't want to talk about it. For once, he didn't, either. Not after hearing Judson's description of Perez and knowing the creep was in the wind and free to strike at a moment's notice.

Detective Wilson was pretty much what Darcie expected of a detective. Broad-shouldered, serious, his focus intense as he offered them disposable booties to protect the crime scene before escorting them into Leland King's house. Sky-high pines and maple trees surrounded the mid-century home with soaring ceilings and a wall of windows that overlooked a wooded ravine.

"Look," Detective Wilson said as he stared at Noah in the entryway. "I'm not sure what you're hoping to find here. I get that you're a big-city detective, and we're small-time to you, but our team was thorough."

Noah held up a placating hand. "I'm not doubting your work. I've found over the years that in addition to searching a victim's home, being there helps me get a better sense of who he is. That's all I'm looking for here."

Wilson nodded firmly.

From Darcie's work with the FRS team and her interactions with the police as a paramedic, she was very familiar with the strong egos of law enforcement officers and she was pleased to see Noah keep this from becoming an issue.

"I'd also appreciate any details and opinions you've formed about the victim," Noah said.

"Not sure we even have a victim yet, but if your hit-list theory is correct then I need to keep an open mind." He held out his hand. "If you'll follow me, I'll show you where we found the blood." Wilson crossed the room, his feet encased in booties that whispered against gleaming hardwood as he walked. He stopped by the white sofa and pointed at a rusty red stain. "Lab tests confirm it matches King's blood type."

Noah stared at the sofa. "Not a large quantity of blood. Could be from a struggle, but it's not enough to suggest murder."

With King's name scratched off the hit list, Darcie believed he'd been murdered, but to hear Noah's blunt statement made her sick inside. She turned her attention to the room to keep her mind off the list.

If she didn't already know King didn't have young children, the room would have told her that. Spotless. Organized. Not a dust bunny in sight. White furniture—with the exception of the blood—was also spotless.

"The prime suspect in our investigation has gang affiliation," Noah said. "Specifically the Nuevo gang. Any chance King is affiliated with a gang?"

Wilson shook his head. "But now that you mention it, I'll be sure to keep a look out for anything related."

"We're also interested in a Ramon Flores. Has that name come up in your investigation?"

"No, should it?"

"His name appears on the hit list we located at our crime scene."

"I see," Wilson said. "So far we've focused on King's personal life to find a possible suspect. Maybe this Flores worked with him, though records indicate this was a one-man operation. We suspect he worked with other designers in his business, but these were online collaborations only and they were paid as contracted staff. I'm working on running down a list of these designers and I'll get the report to you as soon as I have it."

"I'd appreciate that," Noah said.

"It might take some time, though," Wilson said. "Since we don't even know if King met with foul play—he could be in Vegas having a high old time gambling and not taking his sister's calls, for all we know—this investigation isn't my top priority right now."

Darcie didn't like the sound of that and from Noah's frown he didn't, either, but it couldn't be helped. Darcie knew detectives were overworked everywhere and they had to prioritize their cases. It meant she and Noah were going to have to do more of the legwork once they left here.

"What about friends?" Noah asked.

Wilson looked relieved that Noah didn't lecture him on his priorities. "His sister said he was pretty much a loner and didn't have any close friends, just people he chatted with online. His clients were his only real contact with the outside world."

"Then it sounds like his disappearance could be related to his work," Noah said. "I'd like to see his office."

Wilson led them down the hallway to a large room—another immaculate space with huge posters on the walls for what Darcie assumed were recent advertising campaigns designed by Leland. A drafting table sat in the corner and there were plush chairs on either side of a glass table that held a fiery red lamp.

"No computer?" Noah asked, drawing Darcie's attention to the desk across the room.

"We've taken it into evidence," Wilson replied. "Techs are processing it now."

Darcie spotted a 3-D logo on the desk and her heart sank. She pointed at it. "LK Design. Is that the name of his design firm?"

Wilson nodded. "Sounds like you recognize it."

"I do."

"How?" Noah stepped closer.

"Tom—my ex-husband," she clarified for Wilson. "He used this firm to design a campaign for the grand opening of his bike shops." Her legs suddenly feeling weak, Darcie grabbed on to the back of a chair. "I may have even met Leland. He went by Lee, and I'd long ago forgotten his last name so I didn't make the connection before." She turned her attention to Wilson. "Do you have a picture of him?"

Wilson tapped his phone and held out a photo.

"Yes. It's Lee. He came to the grand opening."

"You're sure," Noah asked, his gaze riveted to hers.

She nodded, but she'd already started pondering the connection between a missing man and Tom. Had she let their former life together blind her to the point where she couldn't see Tom for who he was? Was he actually involved in the attempt on her life?

LK Design's full client list in hand, Noah settled into the driver's seat of his car and turned to Darcie to assess her mood. Noah had taken a few moments to process Tom's connection, but Darcie? Questions must be zinging through her head.

He waited for her to make eye contact, then said, "I imagine the news about Tom was a shock."

She shrugged as if it didn't matter, but she looked worried.

"This doesn't mean he had anything to do with your attack," he said, surprised that he was coming to Tom's defense. "We have no reason to believe he has any gang affiliation."

She stared ahead without speaking. Noah didn't want to push her if she didn't want to talk about this, but he would like to help relieve her anxiety if he could. So he waited. Patiently. Letting her take the lead in the conversation.

She met his gaze, and he saw the ragged pain in her eyes before she cleared it away. "What if when I wouldn't sell the house he turned to a shady source for the money? Like a gang. Then he couldn't pay them back and they came after me to teach him a lesson. Or he could have hired someone to kill me. Maybe Alverez."

Noah had thought the same thing, but at this point, it was all pure speculation. "Don't let your imagination run wild. We need to hold off forming an opinion until we have something concrete to go on."

She gaped at him. "What happened to the guy who thought Tom had a role in this? Why are you changing your tune?"

"Honestly?" he said, stalling for time because he wasn't sure he wanted to tell her the truth.

"Yes."

"I can see how painful this is for you. You've been through so much already with Tom and this…" He shrugged.

"Pity again," she said as her lip curled.

"No." He held up a hand. "I don't feel sorry for you. I simply…" He stopped talking because he didn't really know what he felt anymore. "We should get going."

He ignored the hurt look on her face and dropped the client list he'd gotten from Wilson onto the console, then shoved the key into the ignition and got them on I-5 heading back to Portland.

Darcie picked up the list and started flipping through the pages. After rustling through a few of them, she stabbed a finger on the paper and held it out for him. "Here. This confirms Tom was an LK Design client."

Noah glanced at the report to see Bikes on the Go. "Don't jump to conclusions. It still doesn't really tell us anything."

"I know." She set the report on her lap. "It's just…since Haley died and Tom left…" Darcie shook her head. "It's easier to expect bad things to avoid disappointment."

He opened his mouth to reply, but she held up a hand. "And don't offer the platitude that God is in control. That He won't give us more than we can handle. That He knows what's best for us and what to allow in our lives." She tapped her forehead. "I know that up here. I really do. But my heart? The heart that's been shattered by the loss of my child? That's a whole different story."

He'd struggled with the same thing and his pastor had given him sound advice. Maybe he could share it. "Okay, this is going to sound harsh, but I don't know how else to say it. Is there anything worse that could happen to you than losing Haley?"

His statement made her flinch, but she leveled her gaze at him. "Trust me. I've thought about that a lot, and honestly, losing Haley wasn't the worst thing that could have happened. If she'd died without believing in Jesus, that…" She shook her head. "That would have been far worse."

Noah felt the color drain from his face and he looked away before she noticed. He hadn't told her about Evan, but it was as if she'd read his mind and had discovered his greatest fear for his son.

"Not having been through something like this," she continued, "I don't expect you to understand."

"How do you know I've never faced something similar?" he challenged, even though he knew he should just keep quiet.

"I meant losing a child. You've never lost a child."

"I…" he said, but the words wouldn't come.

"Noah?" The genuine interest and concern in her tone made his heart ache. Made him want to talk about Evan. Unburden himself. But he could easily imagine her concern changing to disgust.

He didn't want to see that from her. Would never be ready for that.

His phone rang from the dash—saved by the bell. He glanced at caller ID. "It's Detective Judson with the gang task force."

She sighed out a long breath. "Then you'd best answer."

Noah punched the speaker button, greeted Judson and mentioned that he was on speaker with Darcie in the car.

"Good," Judson said. "Glad I caught you. You'll be happy to hear we picked up Elonzo Perez in one of our sweeps for the Nuevo leaders." Judson sounded hyped up on adrenaline.

Darcie shot an excited look at Noah.

"We questioned him and the other gangsters about Ms. Stevens's attack," Judson continued. "But they all played dumb and lawyered up before we got them in the car."

"So they're not talking," Noah muttered.

"No, but if you're agreeable, Ms. Stevens, we'd like to arrange a lineup. If you can ID the guy as your attacker, then we can hold him while we investigate further."

"Yes," Darcie said with enthusiasm. "Arrange the lineup as soon as possible."

"I was hoping you'd say that," Judson said. "PPB's tactical team made the arrest so the lineup will be at your precinct, Lockhart. How soon can you come in?"

Noah glanced at the GPS. "We're heading back from Eugene, and it'll take us at least an hour."

"Perfect. That'll give us time to get things set up. Call me if anything changes, otherwise I'll see you in an hour."

Noah disconnected the call.

"This could be it." Darcie's eyes lit with excitement. "The end to this nightmare."

"Don't get too excited," Noah warned. "Perez may not be the guy."

Darcie leaned against the door and stared out the window. Noah didn't mean to burst her happy bubble, but he also didn't want to get her hopes up if this didn't pan out. He wanted Darcie to be out of danger more than anything, but for the first time he realized that meant they'd go their separate ways. Something he'd thought he wanted, but now? Now, he just didn't know.

They made the rest of the drive in silence, both lost in their thoughts. When they reached the Portland city limits, Noah radioed dispatch to request a uniformed escort through downtown. The officers would meet them a few miles from the central precinct and form a protective barrier around them.

"We can't risk Ms. Stevens stepping outside," he said to dispatch. "Make sure the officers know we'll be using the sally port." After her confirmation, he disconnected.

Darcie swiveled to face him. "You're scaring me by making this into such a production."

"It's just a precaution."

"But obviously one you think we need to take." Her eyes narrowed. "I don't get why you agreed to let me go to Eugene with you as my only escort, but now all of a sudden we have to up the security."

"This is different." He glanced at her. "The Nuevo gang wouldn't have known about our Eugene trip so they couldn't have planned an attack. But if Perez is really your attacker and he thinks you can ID him, then you can be sure his attorney has told the gang about the lineup."

"They'll know exactly when I'll be arriving and where." Her face paled.

"It's a good possibility," he said honestly. "If you want to reconsider doing the lineup, now's the time to say so."

She shook her head firmly. "If this attack is personal, like Archer seems to think it is, then this creep will keep coming back. If he's not caught, then eventually…" Her words fell off and she shuddered.

"Hey," Noah said. "Remember, I'll be right by your side."

"Thank you." A grateful smile claimed her lips.

He squeezed her hand and turned his attention to the road. They met the patrol cars as planned and the motorcade crept through the busy downtown streets toward the precinct. They hit every light green until a few blocks from Central, where they had to stop.

Feeling like a sitting duck, Noah scanned the sidewalk. A normal day in the downtown area. People walking. Families. Hipsters. Homeless. All mingled together. The MAX train humming past.

The light changed. The lead car started off. Noah advanced through the intersection, then slowed for a jaywalker coming from a tall parking garage.

"Come on, people, use the crosswalk," he mumbled as tension mounted.

They were almost there, and Noah was getting antsy. He kept his gaze running up and down the street. Clear as a bell.

A sudden crash of glass breaking sounded from the roof of his car. Liquid rolled down the windshield.

"Noah!" Darcie clutched his arm. "What's happening?"

"I'm not sure." He stopped the car and craned his neck around to see if he could figure it out.

"Molotov cocktail," the officer to his rear said over the radio. "Get out now!"

Flames trialed down the windshicld and slid under the hood. Darcie reached for her door handle.

"No." Noah grabbed her arm. "Not yet."

She tensed beside him. "We have to get out of here."

"Not yet." He shot her a quick look as panic raced up his back. "This could be a trap. To force us from the car so your attacker can shoot you."

Darcie gasped and looked out the window.

Noah made another visual sweep of the area. No one looked threatening, but a shooter could be in the garage concealed behind a pillar. Rifle at the ready.

Noah didn't know what to do. Did he get out and expose Darcie to gunfire or stay in the car and risk it going up in flames? Either way, she could die.

TEN

The car was hot now. Flames licking all around them. Panic nearly suffocated Darcie. She wanted to bolt from the vehicle, but she trusted Noah. Even if he did look frozen in place.

"Move, Lockhart." The officer's voice came over the radio again.

The voice seemed to spur Noah into action as he grabbed his door handle. "I'll get out first. When you see me leave, you'll want to bail, too. But wait for me to get around the car to your door so I can shield you from any potential gunfire when you get out."

"No," she said. "You can't risk your life like that."

"It's not a risk. You're the target. They won't fire until they can get a clear shot at you." There was an edge to his tone, belying the certainty of his words. He didn't really believe what he'd just said. How could he after the drive-by? They'd fired unrelentingly then, even though he was in their way. Why would this be any different?

He radioed the other officers of his plan, then asked them to provide cover. His gaze lingered on Darcie for a moment. She squeezed his hand and realized how much she'd hate to lose him.

He jumped out and started around the car. Time seemed to crawl by as if he was moving in slow motion. She held her breath. Waited for gunshots to sound. The other officers were out of their cars, heading toward Noah. They wore Kevlar vests, but Noah didn't.

"Please wait for them," she whispered, even though she knew he couldn't hear her. The intensity in her voice scared her more than the fire that was growing larger. "Please. They can protect you."

He hurried around to her side of the car.

Flames engulfed the engine area. Black smoke rose and filtered into the passenger compartment. Darcie took a deep breath and held it. She listened for a gunshot. Waited to see Noah fall to the ground. Worry consumed her. Each second seemed like an hour. A hot, burning, tortured hour.

Help him, Father. Please help him and keep him safe. The other officers, too.

Noah finally reached her. He jerked open the door. Flames licked along the edge of the frame, but he beat them back with his arm, allowing her to exit unscathed.

She smelled burning fabric. Hair. Skin. She knew the smell well from fire callouts.

"Your arm," she cried out as she saw his shirt alive with flames.

"I'm fine." He beat down the flames, then circled his other arm around her back. Drew her close.

"Fall in," he commanded the officers. They surrounded her and the four of them quickly moved down the street to the lead car. Noah whisked her into the backseat and dove in after her.

A mighty explosion sounded behind them, rocking the car. Darcie shot her head around and looked out the back window. Noah's car was engulfed in a fiery inferno now, a total disaster. She vaguely heard the officer climb behind the wheel and request the fire department before he fired up his lights and siren and floored the gas.

She turned backed to Noah. Realized that they had nearly died in horrific flames.

"We could have been in there." Her voice wasn't much more than a whisper.

"But we weren't." Noah moved even closer.

She saw the fabric of his shirt melded with his skin and forgot about what could have happened to focus on what *had* happened. "Your arm. We have to get it treated."

"Not yet." He moved to hide the injury, but cupped the side of her face with his other hand. "Your safety is my only concern. Everything else can wait until you're safely inside the station." He held her gaze and she didn't look away as the driver maneuvered through traffic, making the final few blocks in record time.

The car slammed to a stop and Noah jerked his focus to the window.

"Looks clear," the driver said.

"Then let's move." They quickly escorted her inside the building.

"I'll take it from here," Noah said to the officer. "Let's not let the perpetrator get away this time."

Noah didn't wait for a response and started down the hall, moving Darcie with him. She wanted to make him stop and let her check out his burns, but his steps were feverishly fast. Down the hallway. Around a corner. Into an elevator. The doors closed.

He sighed out in relief. Turned her to face him. Gently pressed her hair from her face. Grumbled something under his *breath*, then took her into his arms, hugging her with a strength she'd known he possessed. He kissed her hair. Kissed her cheeks. Then with a gaze so intense it burned as hot at the flames licking at the car, he settled his lips on hers and kissed her soundly.

She was aware of the softness of his lips, though they were demanding. Almost punishing. She warned herself to push him back, away from her. But when it came to Noah, she had mush where her brains should be. Despite the warning starting to fire in her brain, she wanted the kiss. Wanted it never to stop. She hadn't felt this way in years. If ever.

The elevator dinged, and he jerked back, then almost shoved her away before raking a hand through his hair and stepping into the detectives' bullpen.

He didn't say a word but stormed over to his desk, then gestured at a chair. He was acting mad. Like she'd done something wrong. Like maybe it was her fault they kissed. She didn't sit. Couldn't sit. Not with the adrenaline pulsing through her body.

He pointed at the chair again. She ignored him and remained standing, though her legs were wobbly, and she should probably sink down on the chair before she dropped to the floor. "What's wrong with you?"

He ignored her and picked up his phone. "Lockhart here. You ready for us yet?"

Yeah, he was mad all right. His terse tone made that clear. She stared at him. Memorized everything about him. His rugged stance. His broad shoulders. The way he ignored his injury to continue to do his job. He turned, but didn't look at her, just looked over her head.

She continued to stare at him. At the square jaw that reminded her of his strength. Of his willingness to risk his life for her. She moved to his full lips. The ones that had settled on hers and were ripped away almost as quickly. Too quickly.

She reminded herself that she was here to look at men. Criminals. Hopefully to pick one out of a lineup. And yet all she could think about was Noah and the kiss.

Her gaze fell to his arm. To the seared clothing. The ugly, raised burns that she ached to tend to so she could relieve the pain she knew he had to be feeling. He could have died protecting her. Worry nibbled at her brain. Worry for his safety. Worry that before this was all over he could be seriously, maybe fatally, harmed. That she'd lose him like she'd lost Haley. An ache as sharp as a knife pierced her gut.

She'd let him get to her. Let him find a crack in the fortress she thought she'd locked down. She was starting to have feelings for him. Honest to goodness feelings that she'd never thought possible again.

But it wasn't too late to protect herself. She

wouldn't let that crack widen. Not now. Not with the danger he faced today. Faced every day.

She took a physical step back and a big step in her heart, too. She had to keep things professional between them. She had no room in her life for a relationship—for love. It only led to heartache and suffering. Led to loss. And what worse person to love than a police officer who could die in a heartbeat. That, she couldn't... No! Wouldn't do.

Ever.

Noah paced back and forth outside the viewing room. Pain screamed up his arm, but he didn't care. He'd have it looked at soon. It was Darcie he was concerned about now. She stood before six men and gave off a casual vibe, as if an event like this was no big deal. But it was a big deal. Perez was in that group. Perez, a big, burly man. Tough. Angry. Mean. Maybe the man who'd attacked Darcie.

Judson said something to her and her shoulders slumped. Noah wanted to step in to help. Instead, he curled his fingers into a fist and resisted the urge to ram it into the wall. He had every jurisdictional right to join Darcie in the room, but Judson hadn't wanted him in there. Judson was afraid Noah's presence would distract Darcie. Maybe it would have, but Noah would like to think his presence would also bring her comfort.

Or maybe not. Not after the kiss. He knew it was wrong the minute his lips settled on hers. But he couldn't help himself. Another attempt had been made on her life. He'd reacted. Let his emotions run wild. Then acted like a real bear with her. He'd likely ruined any kind of friendship they'd had.

She suddenly stepped forward and pointed. She'd ID'd one of the men, but which one?

Noah ran his gaze down the line. Eyeing each one. Waiting to see murderous intent. To see the man who did this. To lock him up. To throw away the key.

The door opened. Darcie stepped out. She looked wrung out. His heart creased. He wanted to hold her. To comfort her.

"Is he in the lineup?" Noah asked instead.

Judson stepped in to the hallway. "She ID'd Perez from the day he threatened her at the hospital, but she's not sure he's her attacker."

Noah ignored Judson and focused on Darcie. "It's not him?"

"I don't know." She shook her head as a tear slid from her eye. "I wanted it to be him—how I wanted it to be. But I'm not sure if I just *want* him to be my attacker so badly, or if it really is him." Tears started falling faster. "I'm sorry. I know you were counting on me. But if I can't be positive, then I can't say anything at all."

Noah turned to Judson. "What about an alibi for the time of Darcie's attack? Does he have one?"

"Nothing sound. He claims he was with fellow gang members, who you know will swear to anything Perez says. And before you ask, I went at him for the drive-by shooting, too. Same alibi. Plus he denies knowing anything about the Molotov cocktail. Though mentioning that particular item brought a grin to his face, he's claiming no knowledge." Judson swallowed hard, as if clearing away a nasty taste. "Unfortunately, we have nothing to hold him on now, and we're going to have to let him go."

"If only I could ID him, then this would be over." Darcie bit her lip and swiped angrily at her tears.

Noah couldn't keep his hands off her any longer, but he had to react as any concerned friend might. Not as a man who was interested in her. He rested a hand on her arm and tried to communicate strength and courage.

"We'll get him another way," he said, although, at the moment, he had no idea how.

His phone rang and he wanted to ignore it, but the call could be important. He glanced at the screen and saw Skyler's name. Thinking Darcie couldn't handle any additional bad news right now he stepped away and answered.

"I found a Ramon Flores," Skyler said quickly. "He lives in Veneta, a small town west of Eugene."

Noah let the information roll around in his head. "Leland King's from Eugene."

"Exactly. And Flores has gone missing, too."

Noah glanced at Darcie as she talked with Judson. How was she going to react when he told her that of the three people on the hit list, two of them were missing? She'd assume, as he was doing, that the two men were dead.

"You still there, Noah?" Skyler asked.

"Yeah," he said, pulling his gaze from Darcie so he could focus and do his job. "Tell me about Flores."

"He's twenty-six but he still lives with his parents while he finishes community college. When he didn't come home a few days ago, his parents called County."

"Have you had a chance to check for priors and any gang affiliation?"

"He's clean."

"What about a connection to Leland King? Anything there?"

"Not yet, but I'm looking into it. I plan to give Flores's parents a call after we hang up."

"I got a list of LK Design's clients from Wilson that I can email to you. Maybe you'll see something there."

"What about employees of LK Design?" Skyler asked.

"King worked alone except for contracted designers. Wilson is still working on locating them. As soon as I receive a report, I'll get a copy to you."

"Perfect, and I've asked to have a copy of Flores's case file overnighted to your office."

"At least that's something that might turn up a lead." Noah hated how down he sounded. This could be a solid lead and he needed to grab on to it and hope for the best.

"Something going on that you want to tell me about?" Skyler's voice held concern.

Noah told her about the bombing and the lineup, forcing himself to recount the events like they had no impact on him when they were eating away at his gut.

"Sounds like things couldn't get much worse for Darcie right now."

As Noah thought about Skyler's comment, his hand automatically drifted to his service weapon. "Unfortunately they can. We have no reason to hold Perez so he'll be back on the street in no time."

ELEVEN

Darcie stared at Noah's bandaged arm and the image of his arm engulfed in flames came rushing back. "What did the doctor say?"

Noah offered her a casual smile and dropped into the large recliner in the firehouse family room. "It's no biggie. A little cream and change the bandage on a regular basis, and I'll be good to go."

She was a nurse. An EMT. And she knew he was downplaying the injury for her benefit. "Really, that's all he said? It looked like it might be third degree."

He shrugged. "So where is everyone?"

Darcie didn't miss his change in subject, but she knew he wasn't going to say anything more about the arm so she went with it. "I gave Isabel a bath and Pilar's getting her dressed. Skyler's in the office. I'm sure you ran into Archer in the hallway. The rest of the team is on duty."

He frowned.

"What's wrong?"

"I'd hoped Archer and Skyler would stick closer to you while I was at the ER."

She resisted sighing. "They tried, but I shooed them away."

"I don't like you being alone."

"So you've said, but after the day we had today, I needed time to reflect and pray. Besides, Archer met you at the door, didn't he?"

"Yeah, but—"

"Noah!" Isabel cried out from her wheelchair, as Pilar pushed her into the room. "You're back. I'm going to read to Darcie. Do you want to listen, too?"

Isabel was as excited to see Noah as Darcie had been when he'd returned from his doctor's visit. Darcie hadn't wanted him to go to the ER without her. Partly because she'd wanted to ensure he was getting the best medical care possible, but mostly because she'd been worried for his safety and had wanted him where she could see him. Ha! The shoe was now on the other foot. Not that she thought she could protect him, but at least if he was with her, she'd know what was happening with him.

"Now, Isabel," Pilar warned. "Detective Noah's a busy man."

Noah waved off her concern. "I'm happy to listen."

"And your arm? It is okay?" Pilar asked.

"It's fine." He looked at Isabel. "So tell me where you want to sit, princess, and I'll help you get settled."

"By Darcie." She clutched to her chest a large Bible storybook that she'd brought from home.

Noah scooped her up from the chair and gently settled her onto the thick cushion.

Darcie looked at Pilar. "I'll put her to bed when we're done so you can go on up."

"You are sure? She is taking up so much of your time."

"I love caring for Isabel," Darcie said as she inhaled the sweet scent of Isabel's shampoo. "You never have to worry about that."

"Then good night to all of you." Pilar smiled, but Darcie could see it took effort. At her age, the gunshot had sapped all of her strength and it was taking time to recover. Plus she'd had to care for Isabel while Darcie went to Eugene.

Noah sat back down in the recliner and Isabel squirmed into a comfortable position. Her soft curls tickled Darcie's chin and her warm little body pressed against Darcie's side. Isabel opened the book and placed it across her lap. She flipped to the story of Jonah and his reluctance to do God's will.

Darcie's arm automatically went around Isabel's shoulders and drew her even closer. Darcie sighed out her happiness, drawing Noah's attention. His focus remained on her, but she ignored him and concentrated on Isabel.

"Do you want me to read?" Darcie asked.

"I'll read the first page and you can read the next one," Isabel replied.

She slid a finger along the first line and started the story. They alternated pages as Isabel had requested and Darcie only had to help Isabel pronounce a few words.

At the end of the story, Isabel looked up, her forehead wrinkled. "Did Jonah go to rehab?"

"Rehab?" Darcie asked, trying to hide her disgust over sweet little Isabel knowing about rehab at her age. "Why would he go to rehab?"

"For not listening to God." Isabel scrunched up her face. "*Abuelita* says if I don't listen I could have the same problem as Mommy. She didn't listen to *Abuelita* and took drugs. Now she's in rehab. If Jonah doesn't listen, he might take drugs, too."

Isabel's misunderstanding would be funny if it wasn't so sad. Darcie spent the next thirty minutes explaining about drugs. She felt Noah watching and listening, and despite his intense interest, she found herself enjoying the opportunity to help Isabel. But the time was short-lived as Isabel yawned broadly and her eyes became droopy.

"Time for bed, sweetheart." Darcie closed the book and gently took it from Isabel's hands.

"Will you tuck me in again?"

Darcie nodded as she stood.

"Yay." Isabel scooted off the couch and managed to come to a wobbly stance. She stared at Noah. "Darcie's going to tuck me in." She suddenly lurched forward and threw her arms around Noah's neck.

Isabel bumped his arm and a moment of pain flashed in his eyes, but it was quickly replaced with surprise. His arms came around her back and a look of contentment settled on his face. He was a natural with her, and Darcie knew he'd be a good father. But then so was Tom and look at how that had turned out.

"Let's go, sweetie," Darcie said to Isabel.

She pushed back and planted her hands on the side of his face. "I like you, Noah. You're my friend."

"You're my friend, too, princess," he replied, his voice filled with emotion.

Darcie helped Isabel brush her teeth in the kitchen so they didn't wake Pilar, then maneuvered the girl into her chair and they took the elevator upstairs.

"I like you, Darcie." Isabel threw her arms around Darcie and hugged her hard as she'd done with Noah.

"I like you, too, sweetie." Darcie held Isabel's warm little body and sighed in contentment. Her arms had been empty for so long.

Darcie eased free. "Now we need to sneak you into the bed without waking up your *Abuelita*. Can you be extra quiet?"

Isabel nodded solemnly. Once settled in the bed, Isabel hugged Darcie again. A great longing ripped into Darcie's heart and tears threatened to fall. She eased free before she started crying in front of Isabel. Darcie kissed the child on the nose and pulled up the covers before silently leaving the room as her heart swelled with affection for Isabel and broke for Haley at the same time.

How she missed sharing this closeness with Haley. The bond of motherhood was unlike any other bond. Raising up a child in faith. Being there to share the good times. The joys and happiness. Working through the pain. Skinned knees, friends who hurt feelings and discipline when she chose the wrong path.

All of it. Everything. Darcie had loved it all with Haley. Was loving it now with Isabel.

Back in the condo living room, Darcie's tears started falling in earnest. She wrapped her arms around her waist and slid to the floor, where she tucked up her knees and clasped them hard. She sobbed silently. Deep, racking, pain-inducing spasms of tears. She hadn't cried like this for years. Thought she was over it. Her grief stored away in the neat compartment in her brain.

Why, Father? Why again? Why now?

What was He trying to tell her? Had she not fully accepted her loss? Was her vow never to risk the pain again, never to risk a commitment to another child, never to risk losing that child, really just a way to delay the finality of her loss?

Flashes of her life with Haley flooded her brain. Birth. Baptism. First steps. Growing. School. Her final moments. Lying lifeless, so still while doctors Darcie had worked side by side with performed CPR. Then they had given up. Raised apologetic eyes to Darcie. Her heart had creased so deeply the crevice remained etched like the Grand Canyon. And it would always remain.

She couldn't love again. Not another child. Not another man. Not Noah.

She dried her tears with her sleeve and got up to go back downstairs. She stopped at the door. She couldn't face Noah with blotchy red eyes. With emotions so raw, they felt like a living, breathing thing.

She trudged to the sofa, dropped onto it and pulled up her covers.

No, she wouldn't go down to see Noah when

she was so vulnerable, or he might urge her to move on, when she clearly wasn't ready for such a huge step.

An hour passed and Noah had taken to pacing as he waited for Darcie. He was starting to think something was wrong. She'd never leave him down here without giving him the bedding she stored in her condo during the day, right?

He wanted to race upstairs, but he'd give her more time before intruding. He continued his pacing, stepping back and forth in front of the massive fireplace. Five minutes. Ten. Fifteen.

Still no Darcie.

His chest tightened with concern. Enough. He was going after her. Now.

At the stairway, he grabbed the metal railing without thinking. Razor blades of pain radiated up the nerves in his damaged arm. The doctor who'd treated his burns had offered pain meds, but they were known to cause drowsiness and Noah wasn't about to take them when Darcie relied on his protection.

She needed him. Or maybe he just wanted her to need him…because he'd come to care for her.

The realization him like a freight train, stalling his feet. He thought to deny it, but why? It was better to know about it so he could be on guard around her because nothing had changed.

They couldn't be together. Even if he told her everything and she accepted the way he'd treated Ashley. Accepted that he'd so easily given up his rights to his child. Both big *if*s.

He wouldn't bring another child into this world until he repaired his relationship with Evan and made sure he had a chance to learn about the Christian faith. The way things were going with that, it wouldn't change very soon.

Sure, Darcie claimed she'd never have another child, but he saw her longing tonight with Isabel. Longing that after more time passed would break through her resolve. Then she'd want a child—children—and he couldn't provide them for her.

"So keep your feelings to yourself," he warned himself. "Don't lead her on."

He took a few deep breaths and blew them out. Waited a few more moments until his emotions were back on an even keel, then headed up the steps and tapped lightly on the door in case she was asleep. It wasn't long before he heard her footsteps coming his way. She opened the door and peered up at him with red and swollen eyes.

"I'm sorry I didn't come back downstairs," she said before he could ask. "I'm beat and just want to go to bed."

"I understand." But he didn't. Not really.

Something was up that she didn't want to share with him and it hurt.

"Well, I should…" She jerked a thumb over her shoulder.

"Could I get the bedding for the couch?"

"Oh, right. I'm sorry. How could I forget?" She shook her head. "Hang on, I'll be right back."

She quickly returned and shoved the bedding into his arms like she was shoving him out of her life. Her hand smacked his injured arm.

"Argh," he said before he could control his reaction, then bit down on his lip to ride out the pain.

Her gaze searched his face. "Your arm. I hit it, didn't I?"

"No biggie," he managed to get out when all he wanted to do was shout or hit something until the pain receded. He turned to leave. "Good night, Darcie."

"I'm coming with you."

He spun. "What about going to bed?"

"I want to take a look at your arm."

Her touch, when his emotions were already running high, was the last thing he needed. "The doctor said it's fine and to change the dressing tomorrow."

"Yeah, well…" She crossed her arms and jutted out her chin. "I'm not going to accept that until I've taken a good look at it myself."

"Not necessary," he said and headed down the hall.

She jerked her door closed and caught up to him. Maybe she was experiencing the same needs he was facing. He felt compelled to use his skills to make sure she was safe. Perhaps she needed to use her training to make sure his arm healed.

She took the steps before him and he trailed her down, the echo of their footsteps ringing through the quiet firehouse. She marched into the family room with purpose in her steps and gestured at the sofa.

"Sit," she commanded. "I'll grab my bag from the equipment room and be right back."

With her tone, he didn't even think twice about complying. He dropped the bedding on one end of the couch and sat on the other end. She soon returned carrying a large tote bag.

"Don't tell me I'm going to need all of that," he joked to lighten the mood.

"You'd better hope not or that means you've messed up the arm in record time." She dropped the bag on the floor and pulled up a padded ottoman.

She held out her hand. "Your arm. Now."

"I never knew you could be so bossy."

"Trust me. Living with so many bullheaded guys around, you learn to stand up for yourself real quick." She jiggled her hand. "Come on."

He leaned forward, giving her access to his arm. She gently removed the dressing, but the simple touch further irritated his damaged nerves. To keep it under control, he focused on the top of her head. Several strands of hair had come out of her ponytail and stuck out like porcupine quills. He wanted to tuck them back in. Not something he should, or would, do.

She tsked and gazed up at him with a look his mom had often used when he'd done something wrong. "Some of your blisters have broken and you've soaked through this dressing. Didn't the doctor tell you to change it if that happened?"

"Yes." He didn't tell her it was fine a moment ago because then she would know the jolt from her hand had likely caused the blisters to rupture.

She shook her head and continued to watch him. "Men. You all think you're invincible. You may have mostly sustained second degree burns, but we need to keep on top of them to keep the risk of infection down." She turned her attention back to the burn, her touch clinical, but he could feel the softness of her skin as her fingers brushed against him. His pain disappeared as heat traveled up his arm. He wanted to toss aside the medical equipment, draw her close and kiss her as he had in the elevator.

She suddenly looked up, her cheeks wet with tears. "I'm sorry you got hurt because of me."

"Hey," he said. "It's okay."

"But you keep risking your life for me, when I…" She shrugged and a lone tear rolled down her face.

He looked deeply into her eyes and ignored the need to wipe away her tear. "Don't you know by now that I'd do anything to keep you safe? Anything."

"Yes," she said on a breathless whisper. "And I'm so thankful."

Her eyes locked on his, the raw emotions drawing him toward her like a magnet pulling steel. This thing between them felt right. Good. Natural.

"I wish—" he said and the mere act of speaking broke the spell. They couldn't keep heading down this path or he'd soon have her in his arms. He had to change the subject. Get them talking about something safer.

"So." He blew out a breath. "Do you see a lot of burns on the job?"

Confusion battled with longing in her eyes before a mask of professionalism fell over her face. "More than I'd like, but I treated more burn patients when I was an ER nurse." She resumed working on his arm.

Good. He'd focus on her job. That could work. "You don't see too many nurses as medics."

"No, you don't."

"Ha! Nice job at avoiding my question."

Her head popped up. "I wasn't aware that was a question."

"Let me rephrase. Why'd you leave the ER?"

She frowned and looked back at his arm.

"Guess you don't want to talk about it," he said.

"There's really no big secret. It was simple. I couldn't go back to work in the same place where Haley died."

"But there must be plenty of other nursing jobs."

"There are. It's just…" She shrugged. "I needed a change. Something completely different. Then I got to join the FRS. No better group of people to work with, so I stayed." She finished winding the gauze and sat back. "I'll be asking to see this often."

"That's not—"

"Necessary," she interrupted, finishing his thought. "You decide what's necessary with my attacker, and I'll decide what's medically necessary with your arm."

"Yes, ma'am." He mocked a salute, bringing a grin to her lips.

"It's nice to see you smile." He reached out a finger and before he could stop himself, he ran it over her lips. "I wish I could make you smile more often."

"This isn't a good idea, Noah." She jerked back and started packing up her supplies.

"Don't you ever want to let go of that iron control you have and do what's not good for you?"

"Of course," she said as she zipped her bag closed. "But starting a relationship can only lead to pain, and I've had enough of it to last a lifetime."

"How do you know it'll lead to pain?" he challenged. He had just thought the same thing, but her rejection stung.

"How do you know it won't?"

"Touché," he said, wondering how to continue this conversation. Logically, he agreed with her that a relationship between the two of them would be a bad idea. Yet he couldn't deny the draw he felt, pulling him toward her. Would giving in really be so bad? "Aren't some things worth a little pain?"

"A little pain? Sure. But losing someone you love? There's nothing little about that." She stood and walked away, calling good-night over her shoulder.

He sat back and watched her leave. He didn't have a clue what to do about the way he was feeling. He couldn't even keep things on a professional level with her for five minutes. Then there was Evan. Noah didn't have a clue what to do about Evan, either. The boy had left his social media open for public viewing, allowing Noah to follow his son's life. To see him acting out.

As a cop, Noah had seen this downward spiral many times before. Too many times. If someone didn't intervene soon, Evan was headed for real trouble and Noah would have failed his son yet again.

TWELVE

Noah disconnected his phone call from Judson and headed for the firehouse family room to share the morning conversation with Darcie. Frankly, Noah was getting tired of giving her bad news. He wanted to tell her something to make her smile. Or simply grin and receive that shy, intimate smile that he'd caught from her at times.

Right, like wishing for something would make it happen. If that was the case, Evan would be part of his life, with God in his heart. Maybe Noah wouldn't have given him up, or he would have gone to live with a Christian family.

He found Darcie sitting on the sofa, the red scarf for a fortunate foster child trailing from her knitting needles. Though she said she didn't want another child, she felt compelled to help children. Maybe he could take a page from her book and find a place to work with kids, too, to help him deal with his issues over Evan.

She looked up and let her gaze linger. "Your look says it all. That must have been some phone call."

"Judson was able to read me in on their big investigation." Noah perched on the arm of a chair. "Looks like the Nuevo leaders are laundering money in local motorcycle shops."

"Money laundering. A gang?" She sat forward. "Doesn't sound like typical gang activity."

"Judson said gangs are into so much more than drugs these days. Unfortunately, the shops are legally registered under a shell corporation so Judson hasn't been able to prove the gang connection. They'd hoped their snitch would help, but he died before he could give them what they needed."

"So how will they make their case?"

"That's up to them," Noah said, not wanting to sidetrack the discussion. "What we need to focus on is if, or how, this could be related to your attack."

"I'm not a biker chick, if that's what you're asking me." That grin, the one he often hoped to see, tipped her lips.

Noah laughed and was glad to see she was keeping a sense of humor today. "I simply want you to think if there might be a connection to your attack."

She lifted her head in thought. "There are

motorcycle shops in several of the malls where Tom has stores." She stared over Noah's shoulder and he could almost see the wheels of thought turning in her head. "Kerr Development. Yes, that's it. They're the connection. They own those malls."

Noah thought this was another long shot, but he tried to stay positive. "Could be the connection we're looking for."

"Really? You think this might be about Winnie's sons? Or Tom, even?"

"It's still a reach, but I think it's time that I meet your ex."

Darcie dropped her knitting into a basket. "I'm going with you."

Noah planted his feet. "It's safer for you to stay here."

She stood. "Safer maybe, but you want to get information from Tom, right? He's more likely to talk to me than to you."

"After your last conversation with him, seems like you're the last person he'd want to talk to."

"Maybe, but he's a private guy. He's not going to offer you anything that he doesn't absolutely need to give you." She rested her hand on Noah's healthy arm. "You need me here, Noah. I was married to the guy for ten years. I can read him far better than you'll be able to."

Noah refused to think about the ten years

she belonged to another man, but he couldn't refuse to accept that her help would be invaluable. "There's only one way I'll let you go."

"Name it." Enthusiasm sparked in her eyes and he felt his resolve slipping.

"In case your attacker is watching this place," he said. "We'll have the FRS drive off in decoy vehicles, and I'll smuggle you safely out of here in my car."

"You've got it." She squeezed his arm. "I know Jake's still in his condo and we can arrange it with him."

Noah liked seeing her enthusiasm, but apprehension wove through his mind at the thought of taking her out of the house. "I have a call to make and then I'll be ready to strategize with Jake."

"Perfect." She hurried from the room and Noah went to look out the front window, running his gaze up and down the street as he dialed Bill.

"Yo, Lockhart," Bill answered. "What's up?"

Noah wasn't about to waste time on small talk. "Any word on your background check into Tom Stevens?"

"You're not going to like this. It's just like you suspected."

"What is?" Noah's gut knotted.

"The guy's having serious financial difficulties. He filed for Chapter 11 on his stores. Looks like the reorganization isn't going to fly with the courts and he's heading for bankruptcy."

"So he needs money and needs it yesterday," Noah said as he pondered the implications.

"And we all know money's a powerful motivator to break the law."

And the need for money could lead to money laundering for the gang where Tom could earn some ready cash.

"What about Darcie's background?" Noah asked. "Anything to indicate she was involved with the money issues?"

"Nah, as far as I can tell they've been estranged for most of the last six years, but…" Bill paused, the silence filled with tension. "We've both seen stranger things happen, so you can't rule her out."

Noah didn't for one minute believe Darcie was involved in anything illegal with Tom, but if he was to do his job right, he had to ask. "We're headed over to talk to Tom soon. Maybe he'll help clear things up."

Another longer pause. "Sure you don't want me to talk to Stevens?"

"Thanks, but I've got it," Noah said quickly, knowing full well the situation was far from under control. He was even more vested in Darcie now than when he'd tasked Bill with investigating Tom. But after learning of her ex-husband's immediate financial needs, there was no way Noah was letting anyone else question Tom. No way at all.

Tom crossed his arms, his stance defensive. A stance Darcie had seen many times in their marriage. It meant he was clamming up. If history repeated itself, he'd storm out the door and go somewhere to blow off steam. Maybe back to wherever he'd gone when he'd bailed on her.

He shook his head, then stared at her. "I don't know anything about your attack. Do you honestly think I could be a part of someone hurting you? Un-be-lievable."

"Take it down a notch, Stevens. We have to look at all avenues." Noah's expression held a mix of anger, disbelief and something else Darcie couldn't read. She got that he didn't believe Tom was innocent, even if she did, but she wasn't sure what was causing Noah's anger. Maybe he wanted Tom to be guilty so they could finally wrap up this investigation and get back to their normal lives.

Normal. She didn't even know what that was anymore. "We think this could be gang-related."

"Oh, that's even better." Tom huffed a laugh. "Me involved with gangs. Priceless."

"You know anything about Rocket Cycles down the mall?" Noah asked.

"Puh-lease." Tom rolled his eyes. "You can do better than that, can't you? Everyone knows the shops are operated by the Nuevos. You're trying to connect me to them."

"Is that what I'm trying to do?"

Tom uncrossed his arms and stepped closer to Noah. "Look. I'm not involved with them, but I do see gang members coming and going from the Rocket shops. More in this location than the others. But I don't know what they're up to and I don't want to find out."

Noah moved on. "What about Kerr Development?"

"What about them?"

"How's your relationship with them?"

He paused for a moment and she suspected after his request to sell the house, that he was behind in his rent. "We've always had a positive, professional relationship, why?"

"When was the last time you talked to someone there?"

"I don't know. Last month, maybe. I don't have a reason to keep a record."

"And LK Design?"

"What?" Tom stared at Darcie. "What does Lee have to do with anything?"

She looked to Noah to encourage him to explain his line of questioning. He shook his head.

"What's going on, Darcie?" Tom demanded.

She was caught between them. Her ex and the man she was coming to care for. She didn't have to think long about who would come out on top in this argument. Noah, hands down. At one time, it would have been Tom. They'd been so in love and happy together. They had their share of normal problems, but they'd faced them together. Then he'd left her and filed for divorce, a word she'd never thought would apply to her. But it did. It was her reality now. And yet, here he was asking for her support.

As he'd said, un-be-lievable. She stepped back, telling him he was on his own with Noah. "Just answer Noah's questions. Please."

Tom scowled at her. "Fine, but then I expect an explanation."

"We'll see about that," Noah said.

Tom turned his attention to Noah. "LK handled my advertising campaigns. In fact, Leland was referred to me by the Kerr brothers."

Darcie's mouth dropped open. She didn't expect this connection and had to clarify. "You're sure Kerr Development used LK Design?"

"Yeah, sure. What's the big deal? LK still does their design work."

"But not for you?" Noah asked.

Tom shook his head. "Money got tight and I had to quit advertising. That was a few years ago."

Noah's forehead furrowed. "Have you had any contact with Leland King since then?"

"I haven't seen or talked to him in years."

"You mentioned money getting tight. It's more than tight. You're on the verge of bankruptcy."

Darcie gasped and fired a questioning look at Noah. He'd known about this and brought her here without telling her about it. Did he suspect her of being involved, too? Would he start questioning her next? She now knew how Tom felt in the hot seat and she didn't like it one bit, but she still wouldn't help Tom.

Tom moved closer to Darcie, looking apologetic. "I'm sorry I didn't tell you it was this bad, sweetheart, but I was embarrassed."

"I'm not your sweetheart anymore. You saw to that." Her tone was so harsh and bitter it scared her. She'd thought she'd put this behind her, but just like her loss of Haley, Darcie had to accept that she was still carrying around the baggage. One bag for Tom. One for her loss of Haley. Bags filled with rocks of pain and sorrow that she'd been hauling through life for the past six years.

Tom grimaced and the lips that she'd kissed for years narrowed in bitterness of his own. He stepped closer. "Can we talk alone for a minute?"

Noah shot out an arm, blocking Tom. "She's not going anywhere without me."

They both looked at him. His face colored red and he dropped his hand.

Tom tipped his head at the far wall. "Just over there. For a minute. That's all."

"Fine." Darcie didn't look to Noah for permission as she'd be within his line of sight, but wound her way through colorful bikes to the other side of the room.

Gnawing on his lower lip, Tom joined her.

She shoved her hands into her pockets to keep from crossing her arms. "What did you want to tell me?"

"I'm sorry," he said, sounding honestly contrite. "Leaving you was wrong, but I couldn't stop myself. The pain, our sweet Haley…it was too much. I started gambling. It was the only way to forget. To immerse myself in something so I could pretend life was normal. To go on, you know?"

She totally understood that losing himself allowed him to pretend for brief moments. That's why she'd chosen the EMT job. She could forget her own misery during the intense callouts. Forget as she left the home where Haley had lived to immerse herself in life at the county fire station, where she worked and lived when she was on duty for that part of her job.

"I guess gambling was a better choice than something physically harmful, like drugs or alcohol," she said.

He scowled and shook his head. "There was plenty of alcohol, too, but it's the gambling that destroyed everything and put me so deeply in debt. I'm trying to get my life straight now. Guess I had to hit rock bottom to stop." He leaned closer. "Part of my recovery is to ask for forgiveness. I know I hurt you, Darcie. Hurt you bad. If I could go back and change it, I would. But I can't. I can only hope you'll forgive me for bailing on you like that."

She hadn't forgiven him, that was clear, but could she manage to, someday? She had no idea if he really was in a program to stop gambling, but that was his business. Her business was deciding how to act. Here and now. Today. Did she hold on to the pain from his abandonment or let it go?

Letting go was the right thing to do. For him. For both of them. But could she shed his bag of rocks so easily?

God forgives you for every mistake. The thought came from nowhere. *Why not offer Tom the same opportunity for redemption? And help yourself at the same time. Drop that burden once and for all.*

She could do this with God's help.

"I forgive you," she said, and her heart swelled with emotion as she came to realize that there was honesty behind her statement. She really could forgive him and move on.

"Thank you." Tom's eyes glistened with tears. "I know how hard this is for you."

For a moment, the man who'd hurt her disappeared and she saw the old Tom. The man she'd fallen in love with. Had a child with. She hoped he could move on, too, and wished him well.

"Are you really almost bankrupt?" she asked.

He nodded. "I can hold off for another month or two, but then I'll be…" His despair took the last of his words.

She could help him by selling the house. Could she do it?

Please help me truly to let this hurt go. To help Tom.

The thought of doing so, after so many years of hating him, made her heart soar. They could end things on a positive note instead of with all the bitterness. "I'll sign the house over to you and you can to do what you want with it."

He held up a hand. "I can't let you do that."

"It's time for me to let it go. To move on," she said, feeling light as air. Free. Her heart filled with hope not only for Tom, but for herself, too, for the first time in years.

One of her favorite verses came to mind. May

the God of hope fill you with all joy and peace as you trust in him, so that you may overflow with hope by the power of the Holy Spirit.

Father, please I want Your peace. Your hope.

"We should get going," Noah called out.

Darcie looked at him. Felt the chemistry they'd built. Felt his care and concern. Could she trust God to control her life and let go of her fear of getting hurt again?

Their gazes met. An unspoken connection flowed between them. Her heart fluttered and time stood still, the moment precious and wonderful.

Tom cleared his throat, breaking the link. "If that's all you need, I'll..."

At his voice, the old hurts came rushing back and her defenses sprang back into place. Could she trust another person? Really and truly put all of her past in the past?

"Winnie's waiting for us," Noah said, pulling her back.

She said goodbye to Tom. It felt like a final farewell. A chapter closed in her life. As she walked away, tears threatened to flow and she took a deep breath to hold them back.

"Everything okay?" Noah asked.

"Fine," she said and shut him down. She certainly didn't need to talk about her ex with the man who had found a way to break through her defenses.

They silently climbed into the car and didn't speak again until they headed up the sidewalk to Winnie's home.

"Nice place," he said, looking up at the large, traditional home in the West Hills of Portland.

Two stories with white columns out front and a wraparound porch, the house looked like it belonged in a setting for *Gone with the Wind* rather than in the rustic Northwest.

"It's beautiful, but Winnie's thinking of selling it. She only hangs on to it because her sons were raised here. But now that they've essentially abandoned her, she's ready to let go."

"Like you," Noah said, grabbing her attention. "That was quite a thing you did back there with Tom."

"You heard?"

"Sorry, I didn't mean to eavesdrop, but the room was small." He smiled. "I'm impressed with you, Darcie Stevens. You're one of the strongest people I've ever met."

"I wouldn't say that." She rang the doorbell. "Took me over six years to get to this point."

"So what? You got here and that's all that's important." He frowned. "You inspire me to move on, too."

She wanted to ask him from what, but decided to wait him out and see if he would volunteer his story.

He bit his lip, shuffled his feet, looked down then back up at her. "In college. I was young and foolish."

She laughed. "Aren't we all?"

"Yes, but not all of us make life-changing mistakes."

"What happened?"

"My girlfriend. Ashley. She and I…we—"

The door swung open.

"Oh, good. Ms. Darcie." Winnie's rotund housekeeper of thirty years smiled at Darcie from the open doorway.

Disappointed in the interruption, Darcie forced out a smile. "Good to see you, Harriet."

"The missus has been waiting for your arrival." Harriet didn't linger but went back into the house, her serviceable shoes squeaking on the gleaming marble floors.

Darcie followed her through the impressive two-story foyer with mahogany steps winding up to an open landing. She heard Noah trailing behind her and she wanted to turn. To ask him to finish his story, but it wasn't the right time. She'd have to hope he'd continue it later.

They entered a cozy sitting room, where Winnie sat overlooking a perfectly manicured garden. She started to rise from her favorite chair, but Darcie held up her hand to stop her and rushed across the room.

"My sweet child." Winnie smiled, her eyes crinkling below a cap of silvery curls. "I can't wait to tell you all about my trip."

"And I can't wait to hear about it." Darcie hugged Winnie's fragile shoulders.

Winnie leaned back, looking frail and small in the big chair. Darcie knelt by Winnie's legs that were covered in an old quilt made by her mother.

"Oh, but you brought a young man." Winnie stared up at Noah. "He's a fine-looking one, isn't he?" she whispered. "Is he married?"

"Don't start with the matchmaking again," Darcie whispered back, then turned to beckon Noah over and introduced the pair.

Noah joined them and took Winnie's hand. "Darcie's spoken so highly of you, I feel like I already know you."

"She has, has she?" Winnie eyed Darcie. "This one's usually so quiet you have to pry things out of her. You must be special if she shared anything about her life with you."

Noah glanced at Darcie, and she noticed that his face had colored. His embarrassment over something so simple endeared him to her even more.

"Please sit down, Detective, and tell me what this meeting is all about."

Darcie and Noah both sat, and Noah shared the details of Darcie's attack.

"Oh, my dear, I'm so sorry." Winnie ran her gaze over Darcie. "Are you all right?"

"Yes, and before you start worrying, I have Noah looking out for me."

Winnie's eyes twinkled. "Yes, I see how closely he's looking out for you."

Darcie shook her head, but didn't want to mention Winnie's penchant for matchmaking in front of Noah, so she let it drop. Winnie finally moved her attention to him, her focus sharp and intense.

"So. Let's come right to the heart of your visit, shall we," she said, seeming unaffected by the topic. "You think my sons are upset at me for adding Darcie to my will and they might be involved in these terrible attacks on her."

"It's a possibility," Noah said.

"I can't for the life of me disagree," she said directly.

Darcie swiveled to look up at her. "Really?"

"After what they've been up to, I can't rule it out." Winnie sighed, her disappointment as a mother clearly visible on her face. "Now what else do you need to know, Detective?"

"Would you mind sharing the reason for changing your will?" His tone was gentle and

Darcie made a mental note to thank him for the kindness he was showing Winnie.

"About a month ago," Winnie began, "my accountant told me my sons were involved in moving money to hide losses of underperforming locations. He suspected it was so they could inflate company profits for our annual reports. I spoke to the boys about it. They claimed they were doing nothing illegal, but I don't hold with even a hint of impropriety and insisted they stop."

"And did they?" Noah spoke calmly, but Darcie saw a spark of interest, likely over the close relationship between creative accounting and money laundering.

"They refused, but as the Chairman Emeritus, I have no control of their actions other than to bring it to the board's attention."

"Emeritus?" Noah asked.

"It's an honorary or ceremonial position in recognition of my work in the past, but I have no real standing now." Sadness extinguished Winnie's earlier twinkle. "I didn't want to report them for the scandal it would create. So since money is the only thing they think about, I hoped a change in my will would get their attention and motivate them to mend their ways. All it's accomplished is for them to try to have me declared incompetent."

Darcie took Winnie's papery soft hand. "You can take comfort in the fact that they aren't doing anything illegal."

"Perhaps," she said. "At least nothing they'll admit, or that they've been caught doing."

"I'm afraid I'll have to look into their backgrounds, including their finances," Noah said.

Winnie's expression firmed. "You'll get no fight from me. In fact, unless or until they are successful in having me declared incompetent, I have access to the company's financial reporting system so I'll make sure you have access, too."

"What exactly are you expecting to find?" Darcie asked Noah.

"I'm not sure, but we'll get a forensic accountant to review their books. If they're involved in anything illegal we'll soon know."

Winnie gave a firm nod. "I'd rather it didn't have to happen this way, but they chose this path."

"I hate to ask this, Mrs. Kerr," Noah continued, "but do you really think your sons might harm Darcie?"

"I don't think they would personally attack you, honey." Winnie looked at Darcie, a note of apology in her gaze. "But connections they've established with questionable people could give them access to someone who would hurt you for the right price."

Noah worked his jaw hard. "Then I suggest that at the minimum you bow out of testifying for Winnie."

"Not happening." Darcie crossed her arms.

"He's right, honey," Winnie said. "I can defend myself."

"I know you can and you really don't need me, but I won't back down under their threats. I'm helping you win this battle no matter what your sons might do."

Winnie squeezed Darcie's shoulder, then sat back, looking defeated.

"I'm so sorry this is happening, Winnie," Darcie offered.

"You think you've raised your children right. Raised them to fear God." She tightened her hands into fists. "Then the world, specifically money in this situation, blinds them to their faith."

"I'm sure they'll come around."

"I hope so. And I hope it's quick. I worry about them. About the way they've turned their back on their faith. They know about God… believe in Him. I made sure of that. I honestly don't understand their choices. It's like knowing how to swim and choosing to drown." She shook her head. "Why would they do that? What has money given them? A life of worry, when God's peace is available, that's what. How foolish."

Knowing how to swim and choosing to drown. The words hit Darcie hard and she sat back, stunned. Winnie always retained her peace. No matter her circumstances, she remained calm. She'd weathered storms of health. Loss. Loneliness. And now her sons' betrayal, and yet she always had a smile and a pleasant attitude. Was never rattled and stood unwavering in her faith.

Darcie was just the opposite. She was like the Kerr brothers. She continued to worry. Continued to run from deep, intimate relationships. She was choosing the worry. Choosing to let her loss control her actions. And she'd been drowning.

Slowly but surely.

Day after day for six years. Keeping her head just above water. Ignoring God and His wishes for her life. Ignoring the opportunities to build healthy, happy relationships.

One of these days, oh, yes, one of these days, if she didn't make a change, she was going to sink, and then what?

THIRTEEN

Noah now knew why Darcie liked Winnie so much. She was kind, sweet and wise. Very wise. Her comment about choosing to drown— a priceless nugget. One he planned to give further thought to later tonight when he spent some time figuring out how to finish telling Darcie about Evan. But now he needed to wrap up the interview and then get Darcie safely back to the firehouse.

"I was wondering how involved you are in the leasing of your malls," he said to Winnie.

"Interesting change in topic." She smiled. "I once was very involved, but as I said, I'm more of a figurehead now, attending a board meeting or special event here or there and not involved in the day-to-day business at all."

"So you don't know anything about the vacancy rate at the malls?"

"I do know we have higher than average occupancy." She narrowed her eyes and Noah saw a keen mind observing him, not a woman suffering from dementia. "Suppose you come right out with your question."

"I'm not sure I really have a question, but we've checked into the business, and like you said, you report having a high occupancy rate, but the malls have many vacant storefronts with For Rent signs in the windows."

"Now that I didn't know." She paused. "Doesn't make much sense, does it?"

He shook his head. "And what makes even less sense is when we called the phone number on these signs, we're told that they're not available for rent—that they're already occupied."

Winnie shot a questioning look at Darcie.

"He's right," Darcie said. "After Archer told us about it, I tried calling on a few locations myself."

"Then that is most peculiar." Winnie pursed her lips for a moment, then looked at Noah. "Would you like me to ask my sons about that?"

Noah shook his head. "I'd rather you didn't give them a heads-up that we're investigating them until after we review the company finances."

"Because you think they might try to hide something." She tsked. "I can't say as I disagree." A look of resolve passed over her face.

"I'll make sure you have access to the finances as soon as possible."

"Thank you for your cooperation, Ms. Kerr."

She waved a hand. "Please, it's Winnie. And no need to thank me. It's the right thing to do. Something I hope my sons learn soon."

Noah didn't know how to respond to that comment so he moved on. "One last thing before we go. Do you recognize the names Leland King and Ramon Flores?"

"No, should I?"

Noah shook his head. "How about the company LK Design? Is that familiar to you?"

"Yes," she said. "Yes, I've seen their logos on ad boards they've created for Kerr Development, but again I'm not involved in the daily business so I know very little about the company."

Noah shared a quick look with Darcie. She clearly understood that this confirmed Kerr Development's connection to LK Design. "That's all the questions I have for you, Winnie. Is there anything you would like to ask me?"

She sat up taller, but still looked frail. "Will you please keep me informed of anything you think I might need to know?"

"Of course we will." Darcie scooted closer to Winnie. "Now, tell me about everything you've been up to since my last visit."

Noah wanted to get Darcie back to the safety

of the firehouse, and then delve deeper into the connection between LK Design and Kerr Development, but Darcie needed a chance to escape from the turmoil surrounding her and spend time with her friend. After all she'd been through, that was the least Noah could do for her.

"If you'll excuse me." He held up his phone. "I'll just step out into the foyer to make a few calls while the two of you catch up."

"Afraid of a little girl talk?" Winnie joked.

"Nothing I fear more." Noah chuckled.

On the way to the door, he heard Winnie say, "I like your young man."

"He's not my young man," Darcie replied with a scowl in her voice.

Noah's good mood evaporated. He didn't want to be Darcie's guy, couldn't be her guy, but it hurt to hear her say it. He dug out his phone and dialed Detective Wilson to request all of LK Design's computer files for the forensic accountant to review. Before he could get out his request, Wilson took over the conversation.

"I have bad news, I'm afraid," he said. "We found King's body this morning. A hiker discovered him in a ravine not far from his house."

Noah's heart dropped. He'd expected King's death, but having it made official lent even more credence to the fact that the list found near Darcie's attack was indeed a hit list. "Cause of death?"

"Strangled."

Like the attack on Darcie.

Noah peered into Winnie's sitting room, his gaze lingering on Darcie, where she was engrossed in her conversation with the older woman. For the first time since this had all begun, he saw her smile in earnest and realized how much he would have lost if he hadn't been on his way to Pilar's house the day of Darcie's attack. She could have met with the same fate as King. Become a murder statistic. Her death reported as clinically as Wilson was now reporting King's death.

Worst of all, it could still happen. Especially knowing that King had been murdered. The stakes had been raised, and Noah had to be even more careful now.

"You still there, Lockhart?" Wilson asked.

Noah turned his attention back to the phone. "Do you have a time of death?"

"ME's initial assessment is five days, but you know how preliminary estimates change after the autopsy is performed."

"Which will be when?"

"First thing in the morning."

"If the ME is right, King died the day before his sister reported him missing. Any solid forensics collected at the scene?"

"A few items, but since he was found near a hiking trail, they may not lead anywhere."

Noah had processed enough scenes to know forensic evidence often led nowhere.

Wilson blew out a frustrated breath. "I'll give you a call as soon as the ME has a more accurate time of death and will let you know if we turn up any leads."

"Before you go, I wanted to ask if you've discovered any connection between King and Ramon Flores."

"Oh, yeah—the guy you mentioned yesterday. Nah. Haven't turned anything up, but now that we're dealing with a homicide, I can make the case a top priority."

Noah was glad to hear it. He explained his need for LK's financial records but stopped short of telling him about the money laundering. "If you could upload the files to a cloud server I can retrieve them."

"Sorry. Due to all the recent hacking issues, our department has prohibited online access to any of our files outside of our network. Best I can do is transfer them to a flash drive and overnight that to you."

"That'll have to do then," Noah said, trying

to hide his disappointment as he said goodbye and disconnected.

So how did he proceed? When he got back to the firehouse, he could review Leland King's case file and the LK Design client list. And then, he could spend the rest of the day trying to find any way to connect either LK Design or Kerr Development to the money laundering practiced by the Nuevo gang.

Though he wanted to depart immediately, Darcie was still engaged in conversation, so he caught up on emails and messages until she joined him in the hallway.

Winnie hobbled next to her and came straight to him. "It was a pleasure to meet you, Detective."

"Noah." He offered his hand.

Instead, she put an arm around his shoulder and whispered, "Darcie's worth it, you know. Worth breaking through that armor."

Surprised and unable to form a response, he stared at the older woman.

"If you need my help, come back and visit me anytime." She patted his shoulder and chuckled before hugging Darcie then looking back up at him. "You keep my precious girl safe. You hear?"

"Yes, ma'am," Noah replied to the slight

woman who was tough as nails. "I'll make sure of it."

Once they were in the car, he turned to Darcie. She stared ahead, a line of worry creasing her forehead as she twisted the ring on her pinkie. She was already upset. Hearing about King's death would make that worse, but Noah had no choice. He'd ease into the topic of King.

"It's not hard to see why you're so fond of Winnie," he said.

Her worry faded. "She keeps saying she won the lottery when we met, but really, I'm the one who's blessed to have her in my life. If my mother and grandmother were half as loving as Winnie, my life would have been totally different."

"You really care about her."

Darcie tipped her head. "I never thought much about it, but yeah, I do. She really is like the mother I never had."

"What happened to your mother?"

"Nothing. She's alive and well. But we don't talk much. She had specific expectations for my life, and I never met them. But Winnie?" A genuine smile claimed her lips, and the full force of her warmth, directed at him, sent his heart beating hard. "She's so accepting. That's why it's especially hard to see her sons doing this to her."

"She doesn't deserve it, that's for sure."

"I hate to think about what Archer's investigations of her sons might turn up. Even more, I hate to think about telling her about it."

Noah knew the feeling well, but he had to take the opening. "Speaking of difficult things, I talked to Wilson. Leland King was found strangled, his body dumped in the ravine near his house."

She gasped and clutched her chest. "That's so horrible. I mean, I suspected it was coming, but…"

"There's no way to prepare someone to hear about death," he said and knew he'd struck a nerve when she jerked back. "I'm sorry. I didn't think about hearing about your daughter. I shouldn't have said that."

"No, it's not you. I'm just being overly sensitive. For some reason, this whole thing has brought back the loss of Haley in a way I thought was behind me."

Didn't surprise him, but he was glad she was finally seeing that she still had issues to resolve. If she worked through them, she could be free to have relationships, children. A good thing for her.

Not so good for you. Maybe take a clue from her and figure out your own life.

"We should get going." He cranked the engine and got them on the road. The drive was uneventful until he turned onto the street for the firehouse and the sound of a car squealing down the block had Noah slamming on his brakes while his awareness shifted into high alert.

Darcie shot him a look. "You don't think that's them again, do you? The shooters?"

"Maybe." Searching the area, he pulled to the curb.

Tat. Tat. Tat-tat-tat. A machine gun's rapid fire broke through the neighborhood quiet.

"Machine gun," Noah mumbled.

Darcie grabbed his good arm. "The firehouse. Could it be coming from there?"

"Yes," he admitted, though he wished it wasn't true.

"We have to get over there."

"No," he said firmly as the gunfire escalated. "I won't put you in the line of fire."

"But the team, Pilar and Isabel. They could need us."

"Pilar took Isabel to the doctor and shouldn't be back yet."

"And the team?" Panic took her voice high. "What about the team?"

Yeah, what about them? The brave men and women who might need him? His fellow law enforcement officers that he was letting fend for themselves? But he could do nothing for them without risking Darcie's life. "They're professionals. They can handle this."

"But still, they need us." Her gaze darted around as if she was looking for a way to bail on him.

He met her gaze and held it. "What can you do to help them that they can't do for themselves?"

"If they're injured, I—"

"You what? Will battle through flying bullets to tend to them?"

"Yes."

He gently tapped her forehead. "Think with your brain, not your heart. If we pulled into the firehouse parking lot, it would distract your friends and that would put them in more danger."

"But we can't just sit here." She stared at him in disbelief. "We have to do something."

"We *are* doing something. We're staying put."

She crossed her arms and sank down on the seat. If they weren't in such danger, Noah would laugh. She acted all tough and said she wasn't one to get involved with others and here she was willing to run through bullets for her team.

He turned up the volume on his police radio and questioned the dispatcher about the incident. They reported that the FRS was pinned down in the firehouse by two shooters in a car fitting the same description of the one used in the earlier drive-by shooting.

"It's him," Darcie cried out. "It really *is* him. He's there. My friends are suffering and I'm not there to help them."

He met her gaze. "Don't take this on yourself."

"But I—"

"But nothing. You have done nothing wrong. It's all on the shooters."

Sirens sounded in the distance, taking her attention and providing Noah with a slim sense of relief.

"Backup's on the way, Darcie. They'll be fine," he soothed, but his gut remained tied in a knot for his fellow officers. He'd come to like and respect all the members of FRS even more over the past few days. He hated the thought of anything happening to them.

A responding officer reported the suspects fleeing in their car south on the very road where Noah had parked. If the shooter recognized Noah's vehicle, he and Darcie would be sitting ducks. Odds were that they didn't know the make of the new car Noah was driving, but odds hadn't been in their favor thus far.

He watched ahead, waiting. The car came charging toward them. Three men inside. Windows open. Noah continued to watch, hoping to make out a face, but they sped by too quickly. Still, it was good that they didn't recognize Darcie or they would have fired on her again.

She dug out her phone. "I'm calling Jake."

"No," he said sharply to stop her. "Not until we hear an all-clear on my radio."

"You think there are others who might keep attacking the firehouse?"

"No, but just in case, we can't take their attention when they might still need it. Our need to know how they're doing comes secondary to their safety." He took her hands. Icy cold and clammy. "You know that, right? You've been in situations like this with the team?"

"Yes, but I've always had Jake calling the shots. I can trust his instructions to always be right."

"And you don't feel that way about my directions?" For a moment, he couldn't think of anything except how much her words hurt. "You don't trust me."

"I do, it's just…" She shrugged and slipped her hands free. "I don't know you as well as Jake. Our team has been through so much with him, and we've always come out the other side."

"And we haven't been through tough situations? Your life has been threatened and I was there, right? By your side." He firmly met her gaze. "And as long as you're in danger, I'll never walk away. Never." *Not like your ex. Not as I did with Ashley.*

"You *will* be there, won't you?" she asked, as

if for the first time she realized how committed he was to her safety.

She lifted a hand and gentle fingers settled on his cheek like a kiss. "I trust you, Noah. I really do."

Even if he could come up with a response, the surge of emotions he felt when he looked into her eyes, liquid with emotion, made it hard to speak. The urge to sweep her into his arms was as tangible as the pull between them. He reached for her hand instead. Took it. Twined his fingers through hers. She pulled her gaze away to look at their hands.

"Darcie," he whispered, hoping she would look at him and he could find a way to talk about Evan. Tell her that he was falling for her and hope that she would understand his past.

The all-clear came over his radio, and she jerked back. "We should go. They might need me."

"You're right." He shifted the car into gear and knew something had shifted between them, too.

They'd forged a bond of trust and without words, they'd communicated an acceptance of the interest burning between them. Another step in bringing them closer together. The last thing either of them needed.

FOURTEEN

Darcie held her breath as Noah drove through the yellow crime-scene tape fluttering around the perimeter of the firehouse property. He'd said he wasn't letting her out of the car in the street, so he'd gotten special permission to drive into the back lot that, though it hadn't seen any action, officers had cordoned off. Several officers were standing duty there.

He parked and turned to her. "Your attacker would be foolish to try anything with the extensive police presence, but stay close by my side, just in case."

Memories of the shooting at the precinct came rushing back and he didn't have to tell her twice. She would gladly stay close to him. He got out, and she waited for him to open her door. The minute she exited, his arm went around her waist, drawing her tight against his hip. His posture was rigid, his expression closed, but his eyes were focused, and he stepped with purpose around the side of the building.

Her first look at the firehouse brought a gasp to her lips. Cops swarmed over the area like a disturbed hill of angry fire ants. Bullet holes riddled the building. The shooters had literally sprayed the first-floor exterior from top to bottom, and bullet holes peppered the beautiful antique fire doors. Tears pricked at her eyes as she searched for her team. Jake stood outside along with Brady, who had his sniper rifle casually slung over his shoulder.

She forgot all about Noah's directions, broke free and ran to Jake. "Is everyone okay?"

"Fine. I'm glad to see you're okay, too." He hugged her hard before setting her free. Jake was always the picture of professionalism whenever he was on duty. If he thought to hug her in front of the sheer volume of police officers in attendance, he had to be very unsettled and that raised her anxiety even more.

"We should get you inside," Noah chided her, along with a look that said *I told you to stay close by.*

The anxiety she'd barely kept under control broke free. "Why? Because it's so safe in there?" She gestured at the door. "Look at this. Anyone sitting in the family or game room would have died." She shuddered and a dam of tears burst.

Jake stepped forward, but Noah beat him to her side. He drew her into his arms, and she let him hold her. Right here in front of everyone. She didn't care if she seemed like a weak, weepy female. She'd been choked, shot at, bombed and now they'd open fired on her friends, too. If that didn't deserve a good cry, what did?

Noah pulled back. "C'mon, honey. We'll go inside and the rest of the team will join us soon, right, Jake?"

"Right," Jake replied.

With a warm arm around her shoulders, Noah guided her through the chaos. Under normal circumstances, she'd shrug off his touch and take time to analyze that he'd just called her honey. But now, her entire focus needed to stay on the latest shooting.

They stepped into the foyer and she cringed at the extensive damage to the place she'd called home for the last six years. "Why do they keep trying this whole drive-by thing over and over? Don't they realize it's not working?"

"Gangs work on the dumb-luck theory. If they keep trying it, they figure that at some point they're going to hit their target."

His comment struck like a knife to her chest and she jerked back.

"Hey." He cupped the side of her face. "I know that was blunt, but you want the truth, right?"

"Yes." She shuddered. "But this truth is almost too hard to handle."

"Just hang in there a little longer. We're going to end this today."

"End it today? How? We don't have any solid leads."

"I'm going to arrange a safe house for you with round-the-clock protection until we catch whoever's behind these attacks."

Darcie glanced around the space. Bullets had lodged in drywall and chipped off concrete. She wasn't one to run, but she suddenly liked the sound of a safe place. For her. For the others. *Isabel and Pilar.* "I'm not going anywhere without Isabel and Pilar."

"No problem. They can come with you."

She gestured at the tattered space around them. "After seeing this, I won't argue."

"We'll pack your bag and I'll make the arrangements."

"Isabel and Pilar will need to pack, too."

"I'll go tell Jake to send them upstairs as soon as they arrive." He turned to leave.

Darcie stopped him. "Thank you for keeping a level head and making me wait in the car. If I had come over here in the midst of the gunfight…" She shook her head.

"No biggie."

"I don't know what I'd do without you," she

said, and she meant it. Boy, how she meant it. Not only in regards to her safety, but also in regards to her life.

She was getting used to having him around, and she'd honestly miss being with him when this was all over.

The safe house with very few windows was quite serviceable in Noah's opinion. Sure, it was blandly decorated, the furniture was sparse and basic and the heavy blinds to keep people from looking in meant that the place seemed dark and cave-like.

It was, in one word, safe. And that was all that mattered to Noah.

Archer was too busy checking the windows and doors to seem to care about the decor. Darcie and Pilar seemed less impressed. Pilar ran her finger over a table, checking for dust, and Darcie stood in the entry as if not wanting to step deeper into the house. Isabel, now in a cast that allowed her to walk, limped into the family room and frowned at the ancient television.

Noah's best bet was to ignore their unease and try to make the stay there as enjoyable as possible. "The bedrooms are down the hall. You can choose the ones you want."

"Yippee." Isabel hobbled toward the rooms.

"I'd better go with her to make sure she

chooses wisely," Pilar said, already heading across the room.

"You should choose one, too," he said to Darcie when she didn't move.

"What about you?" she asked him. "Don't you need a room?"

"I'll be on duty most of the time. When I'm not, I'll catch a quick nap on the sofa."

"We could call in more of my team members to rotate standing watch so you can get some sleep."

He met her gaze and held it. "The more people coming and going, the greater chance that your attacker will find this place. Plus, I doubt I'll be able to sleep much anyway. Not with all of your lives on the line."

She stepped closer. "You seem to be taking this personally."

"It is personal. Don't you know that by now?" He ran a gentle finger over her cheek, before forcing himself to step back. "I'm heading out to meet with Winnie's sons. Is there anything else you need before I go?"

She shook her head, but seemed sad that he was leaving.

Noah didn't want to go, but he believed he needed to question the Kerr brothers personally so he could look them in the eye and assess their truthfulness. Besides, Darcie was safe here. *If* she followed his directions. "Promise me you'll stay inside and listen to Archer."

"I will."

"All the time, Darcie. Not just when it suits you."

She watched him for a few moments. "Your comment stings, but I deserve it. I've argued with your directions plenty of times. I've tried not to, but—"

"But you won't depend on a man again."

"I'm that obvious, am I?"

"Tom hurt you. I get that you're gun-shy, but is that how you want to live the rest of your life?"

"Honestly?"

"Yeah, honestly."

She nibbled on her lip for a moment. "I thought so. Until this week. Until I spent more time with you."

"And now?" he asked, holding his breath in wait for her answer.

"Now I don't know." Her lips tipped in a sweet smile. "I guess I'm on the fence about it."

He wanted to ask what it would take to move her to his side of the fence, but he had no right to ask that of her. Not until he dropped his bombshell. "There's something I need to talk to you about when I get back. Will you make some time for me then?"

"It's not like I can say no. There's nowhere I can go to get away from you." She chuckled.

He smiled but he didn't really feel it. She joked, but he wondered if she was just trying to lighten the mood or if she really didn't want to talk to him. It was becoming more and more important for him to know how she felt about what he'd done and he was going to tell her about Ashley and Evan tonight if it was the last thing he did.

FIFTEEN

Randall and Michael Kerr sat at the polished mahogany table in their posh conference room on the top floor of their high-rise office building. Noah remained standing as he questioned them about LK Design. The pair clearly looked down their noses at Noah, but if they thought that would intimidate him, they were wrong.

"Why all the questions about LK?" Randall crossed his legs, leaving a crease in otherwise perfectly pressed khakis. "Is the business in some sort of trouble?"

"Leland King is missing," Noah said and waited for a response.

"Missing." Michael shot to his feet. The oldest of the brothers, he was tall and thin with nondescript brown hair and wore a perfectly tailored gray suit. "How? What happened?"

"I really can't share details of the investigation, but his sister reported him missing."

"And you think we might know where he is

or be involved with his disappearance? Preposterous." Randall stared coolly at Noah, a cold, sharp gaze that probably served him well in the business world.

Noah didn't like this guy, but unfortunately for the investigation, he believed that the brothers weren't involved in King's death. Still, Randall was nervous about something as he fidgeted with the collar on his polo shirt.

"Have you checked with Ramon?" Michael asked and turned to his brother to share a worried look.

"Yes, Ramon. Good idea," Randall chimed in as he often had after Michael looked to him for confirmation. "They work very closely together. If anyone knows where Leland might be, it's Ramon."

They had to be referring to *the* Ramon Flores on the hit list. Noah schooled his voice to play down his interest. "Ramon who?"

"Ramon Flores," Randall replied. "Leland's top freelance designer."

"He was more than that." Michael ran a hand through his hair, leaving tufts standing. "Leland was also Ramon's teacher at the community college a few years ago. Plus he's serving as a mentor for Ramon while he finishes his schooling."

Interesting. Very interesting. Ramon and Leland *were* connected. Something that, given time, he suspected Skyler would have discovered in her research.

Noah needed to know more about this guy. "Did Ramon work out of Leland's home office, too?"

"Not sure if he worked there," Michael said. "But he was often hanging around when we met with Leland."

Randall nodded. "We never really interacted directly with Ramon. Leland said he wasn't officially associated with the firm but was an independent contractor."

"I'm surprised Ramon wasn't the one who reported Leland missing." Michael eyed Noah. "Is Ramon okay?"

Hardly. "We're focusing on King."

Noah could see the brothers didn't miss his non-answer and were about to ask additional questions so he decided to quickly change the topic. "Your mother tells me that that two of you have been involved in a bit of financial maneuvering."

Randall rolled his eyes, then glanced at his brother. "As we've told her over and over again, we aren't doing anything illegal. She has a vivid imagination spurred by her dementia."

Noah made strong eye contact with Randall. "She didn't seem to be confused or suffering from dementia when I spoke with her."

"She has good days and bad days," Michael said. "You must have caught her on a good one."

Noah doubted it. He'd seen people with dementia and even when they had good days, some confusion lingered. Not so with Winnie and he hated to see these young men speak so poorly of their mother.

"Where do you think she got the impression that you were involved in underhanded activities?" Noah asked.

"She probably got suspicious when she learned about the attorney we hired to help manage the company's finances." Randall shared their well-known attorney's name. "We simply hired him to learn effective ways to minimize our tax liabilities on company profits, but he's represented clients who've been found guilty of tax evasion so he's gotten a bad rep."

"I've heard of him," Noah said. "He and his associates go beyond questionable to sleazy."

Randall crossed his arms. "That's your interpretation, but our attorney has never been implicated in anything illegal."

Noah assumed these were the unethical men Winnie mentioned. Noah would find pictures of the attorneys on the internet and show them to her for confirmation.

He turned his attention to Michael. "You rent several of your retail spaces to Rocket Cycles."

"We have a few leases with them, yes."

"So you're in regular communication with the Nuevo gang, then?"

Michael jutted out his chin. "First of all, there's no proof that the Rocket stores are owned by any gang."

Noah snorted.

Michael crossed his arms. "If you're so sure about the connection show us the proof."

The answer didn't surprise Noah. The Kerrs' lawyers likely investigated Rocket before signing a lease with them so they could disavow all knowledge of the criminal connection. "What about money laundering?"

The brothers shot a quick look at each other, and Noah would have to be blind not to catch the guilty surprise in their expressions.

Randall's chin went up and he looked very much like a larger, tougher version of his mother. "If Mother has accused us of that, she truly has gone off the deep end."

"As we've said—" Michael planted his hands on the table "—we've done nothing illegal. That's all you need to know. If you have further questions please direct them to our attorney. We're done here."

Noah couldn't force them to talk to him or answer any additional questions, so he let their secretary escort him out of the building. In his car, he dialed Archer to check in on the safe house.

"Everything okay?" Noah asked.

"We're all good." Archer said. "And as a bonus I have some news on the Kerr brothers."

"They're involved?"

"Maybe." Noah heard papers shuffling. "I used the online access from Winnie and did a preliminary search through Kerr Development's recent financial records. I discovered someone is paying exorbitant monthly rents on the vacant properties. I don't know if they have official leases as I don't have access to their legal paperwork. I *can* see that rents are currently paid by a subsidiary of the shell corporation that owns Rocket Cycles."

"Interesting," Noah said as he digested the information. "So why are the buildings empty?"

"I have more work to do to prove this, but I believe that the Kerrs are indeed laundering money for the Nuevos and leaving the properties vacant allows their scheme to work."

"How?" Noah asked excitedly.

"Kerr Development has a very generous program in place for their lessees who refer a potential client to lease vacant spaces. In a given month there are hundreds of referrals paid out, but—" he paused and Noah tapped his foot in wait for the information "—all of the paid referrals thus far have gone to one corporation only. The same shell corporation that owns Rocket Cycle."

"So let me get this straight. This subsidiary pays rent on all of these properties and then Kerr Development pays it back to Rocket as a reward for client referrals."

"Yes, but Kerr also keeps a hefty portion of these inflated rents. It's a win-win. They make money and the shell corp gets clean money that they can then legitimately spend."

"You're right. It's a classic case of money laundering."

"And if the Kerr brothers are guilty of money laundering with the Nuevos, then it isn't too much of a stretch to imagine they are in deep enough with the gang to order a hit on Darcie so they don't lose their inheritance."

"And the Nuevos would be happy to comply because if Darcie inherited a controlling interest in Kerr Development, the Nuevos money-laundering source would dry up."

"Exactly," Archer said and let the word hang there for a moment. "You think this is what Judson meant when he mentioned the Nuevos's money-laundering scheme?"

"Only one way to find out," Noah said. "I'll give him a call. If our theory is right, and he wants evidence, how long before you have this locked down?"

"I should have it by the morning if I pull an all-nighter."

"Then pull the all-nighter. I'll even make the coffee to keep you awake." Noah laughed. "I'll call Judson and come straight back to the safe house to update you."

Noah disconnected and immediately dialed Judson. He answered on the third ring.

"Hold on a second." Judson put Noah on hold before he could get his story out.

This call was so important, Noah couldn't sit still in the car. He got out and walked the perimeter of the parking lot. The crisp, cold air brought his thoughts into focus. This could be the lead they needed. The lead that would end these attempts on Darcie's life so they could all go back to their own lives.

He absolutely had to tell her about Evan tonight. His gut tightened with that all too familiar worry. Just the thing Winnie talked about earlier. He was letting life take over. Drowning, as she'd said. He was choosing to ignore God and forget that He was bigger than Noah's circumstances. God could find a way for Evan to know Him. And a way for Darcie to understand his past. Noah just had to trust.

"Okay, Lockhart," Judson said as he came back on the phone. "What did you need?"

"It's not what I need. It's what I can offer to help you." Noah relayed Archer's information.

"And your guy has proof of this?" Judson asked.

"Yeah," Noah replied. "At least he will by morning."

"Then get it to me ASAP and we'll bring the Kerr brothers in and have a run at them. Maybe we'll solve both of our problems at the same time."

Not more than five hours later, Noah stood before Darcie in the safe house living room. She sat on the sofa, a soft smile on her face, looking expectantly up at him. Archer had located concrete proof of the Kerr brothers' money-laundering connection to Rocket Cycles and delivered it to Judson. The DA would review the information tonight. If he thought they had a prosecutable case, officers would pick up the brothers first thing in the morning.

A cause for celebration for everyone but Winnie. Noah couldn't celebrate anything. Not when Darcie didn't know about Evan.

Noah drew in a deep breath to start his story, but a familiar thread of worry wove through his gut.

Remember. If God wants Darcie to look favorably on you, then she will.

Please, Father, Noah prayed though the time for praying was over and the time for acting was upon him.

"I don't know how to start so I'll just blurt it all out," Noah said as he paced across the small room.

Darcie's smile evaporated. "You're scaring me."

He had so much to lose here that he could barely continue to meet her gaze. "I have a son," he began. "My college girlfriend got pregnant."

"Wow!" Darcie fell back against the sofa and stared at him. "I can't imagine—"

"I know this is a bombshell," he interrupted. "But please let me tell the whole story before you say anything more. Okay?"

"Okay," she said, sounding cautious.

"So like I said, Ashley got pregnant. We were sophomores. Just barely nineteen. Way too young to be parents. But there we were. Five months from having a child." He shook his head and couldn't speak as the panic from the day Ashley had told him about the baby came rushing back.

"So what did you do?" Darcie's voice was a breathless whisper that he couldn't begin to evaluate when he so wanted to know what she was thinking.

"Nothing," he admitted.

Her mouth fell open and he had to pull his gaze away.

"I did nothing," he continued. "I didn't support Ashley. Didn't help her figure out what to do. Didn't even tell my parents. I just blocked her and the baby from my mind and went about my life at college as if it never happened. Started drinking a lot to help forget."

Darcie crossed her arms and sat back. "You abandoned her?"

"Yes," he said, but it was barely audible.

Darcie's eyes narrowed. "What about Ashley? What did she do?"

"She dropped out of college to have the baby, then asked me to sign over my rights when the baby was born, which I did without blinking an eye. Her parents have been raising him. His name's Evan. He's fifteen." Noah glanced at Darcie and saw nothing in her expression that told him what she was thinking or feeling. "Once I knew her parents had custody of Evan and that he would be raised in a safe, stable home, I came to grips with it all and went on with my life for a long time."

"So you're saying you're okay with what you did?"

"Okay with it? No. I shouldn't have given Evan up before knowing if I really could handle being a parent. I should have stood by Ashley and tried to be a dad, or at least helped her decide what would be best for the baby, whether it was us or not."

"And now? Do you want to have a relationship with him?"

"Yes, of course. In fact, I recently learned Ashley's parents turned away from their faith when she got pregnant and they haven't raised Evan to know the Lord."

A look of disapproval crossed her face. There, finally, was the judgment he expected.

"I want to change that," he rushed on. "I've tried to change it. After I found out, I approached Ashley's parents. They won't let me have anything to do with Evan."

"And so you gave up?"

He shoved his fingers into his hair in frustration. "What else am I supposed to do? I can't go against their wishes and talk to Evan. That would be wrong for everyone."

"Got some news for you," Skyler said, charging into the room.

Noah wanted to ask Skyler to take a hike. To continue his discussion with Darcie and see, once and for all, how this changed things between them. But Darcie's expression and last statement said it all. She couldn't fathom how someone could act the way he had.

"This is a bad time." Skyler backed to the doorway.

"No," Noah said. "It's fine. What do you have?"

"Two things." Her gaze moved back and forth between the two of them before she cautiously stepped forward. "First, I finished my investigation into Mayte. She had gang affiliations, but I found no connection to the Nuevos so I doubt she's involved in this situation."

"That's good news," Darcie said, sounding sad.

"You don't sound like you think so."

"No, I...it's good." She forced a smile. "What's the second thing?"

Skyler arched an eyebrow. "Not such good news, I'm afraid. Ramon Flores's body has been found, too."

"Let me guess," Noah said. "Strangled."

"Yes. He was found in his car. It was pushed into a ravine near a lake and a fisherman came upon it."

"Is that all?" Darcie asked, looking exhausted by everything.

Skyler nodded.

"Then I think I'll go to bed." Darcie stood. "Thanks for your help, Skyler, but I've had enough bad news for the day. Hopefully when I wake up the Kerrs and whoever they hired to attack me will be in jail and *all* of this will be over."

She let her gaze linger on Noah before she left the room, her expression still blank and unreadable.

"What happened to the happy Darcie we saw a few minutes ago?" Skyler asked Noah.

"She'll be back after a good night's rest," he said and hoped that wishing for such a thing would make it a reality.

SIXTEEN

The next morning, Darcie wanted to go with Noah to the interrogation of Winnie's sons. Of course, Noah said no. Darcie understood, but she'd thought the car ride would have been a perfect time for them to continue last night's conversation. He'd have to listen to her and couldn't walk away when she came near, like he'd been doing all morning.

She didn't blame him for avoiding her. She'd let him down. Let him believe she thought badly of him. Well, actually, she *had* thought that way. Last night anyway. When he'd blurted out his story, all she could think about was her precious daughter and how she would do anything— anything!—to hold Haley again. She couldn't fathom a person who would give up their child as easily as Noah had done.

But then this morning as she'd watched Isabel, Darcie realized how much better Isabel's first years would have been if Mayte had recognized that she couldn't care for Isabel and had either given custody to Pilar or put Isabel up for adoption. If Noah, as a teenage boy, not yet a man, hadn't thought he could be a father, then he was probably right that he shouldn't have been one.

She didn't condone the way he handled it, the way he walked out on Ashley, but again, he was young. Naive. All she had to do was think of the things she'd done at nineteen and she could understand. Especially when it was perfectly clear how much he regretted it.

Plus, it didn't mean he was that kind of man now. If he bailed when things got tough, he'd have been long gone a few days ago. But he'd stood by her side, giving everything, and even showing his willingness to give up his life. For her.

Now all she wanted to do was find a way to help him reconnect with his son because she could see how much he was hurting. He'd lost his son, just as she'd lost her daughter. The circumstances were different, but the emotion was the same.

"Watch me, Darcie, I can run," Isabel called out as she slowly hobbled across the backyard toward the neighbor's fence, likely chasing another hummingbird as she'd been doing all morning.

Darcie waved and smiled.

Finally, Isabel was having fun. Darcie had

been doing her best to care for Isabel while Noah was at the precinct so Pilar could get some rest. Usually caring for Isabel was a breeze, but today had been a challenge. She grumbled about everything. Unusual behavior for the often-cheery child.

Darcie suspected Isabel was picking up on the tense atmosphere in the house. Maybe flashing back to her life with Mayte. They'd had to move around frequently then, too. And then there was Pilar. Her arm was healing well, but she'd been exhausted despite resting for hours on end. Darcie suspected the exhaustion was from trying to raise a rambunctious six-year-old in the later years of Pilar's life. Darcie honestly didn't know if Pilar was capable of managing the daily tasks of motherhood on a long-term basis.

And here Darcie stood worried for both of them. For Noah. For Winnie. She wouldn't worry if she didn't care so much. So, fine, she'd let herself become attached to them. All of them. Just like she'd gotten attached to her FRS teammates. It was no secret that she cared about them. She just didn't know how much until yesterday's shooting.

And Noah? How much had she let him in?

She shook her head and stepped across the yard. She'd put herself in the very position she'd said she'd never be in again and she had no idea what to do about it. Six years of self-protecting instincts told her that once this was all over, she should walk away from it all before she lost one of them.

But wouldn't leaving them be just as bad as losing Haley? No. She'd know they were alive and well.

"You wouldn't have to grieve," she told herself when she knew it was a big fat lie. She'd grieve their absence in her life. And it would be her own fault—her choice to leave them behind.

"Darcie." Isabel spun, her smile wide, her eyes alight with joy. "Hurry. Look it's a puppy."

A big fat lie, all right. She'd certainly grieve the loss of connection with Isabel, who was holding a wiggling furry white puppy on her lap. The puppy's pink tongue lapped in an effort to connect with Isabel. She was giggling hard and Darcie's heart lit with happiness.

She knelt by the pair and scratched the dog behind the ears. "Where'd you come from, little fella?"

Isabel pointed at a gap under the fence. "Can we keep him?"

"I'm sorry, but he probably belongs to the people next door."

"Aw." Isabel's lower lip popped out. "I want him. He's fun."

"I know, sweetie, but we need to return him

before his owner gets worried." Darcie took the puppy and stood.

Tears formed in Isabel's eyes, breaking Darcie's heart. "C'mon, sweetie. Let's go inside and we'll find something fun to do while Archer takes the puppy home."

She sniffled but let Darcie help her to her feet. "Can I carry the puppy?"

"Sure," Darcie said, though she knew the longer Isabel held the puppy the more she would want to keep him.

Just like the longer she spent with Noah, the more she wanted to keep him in her life, too.

Argh! Focus on something else.

She concentrated on getting Isabel up the steps to give the puppy to Archer so he could return it to the neighbors.

While he did, Darcie did her best to distract Isabel. "You said you'd like to learn to knit. Would you like to learn now?"

"No." She looked down at her feet.

"How about we read a book?"

"No."

"A game? We could play Chutes and Ladders," Darcie said, mentioning one of Isabel's favorite games.

"No."

"What would you like to do?"

"Nothing." Her lip came out again.

Darcie retrieved Chutes and Ladders and set it up in hopes of enticing Isabel to play. It soon worked and they'd started the game when Archer returned with the puppy in his arms and a bag filled with dog items.

"Puppy!" Isabel screamed and ran to him.

"You were supposed to return it," Darcie said.

"I tried, but then I kept thinking about how happy it made Isabel so I asked the neighbor about maybe keeping him. He said the pup's part of a purebred litter, but this little guy doesn't have the markings necessary to sell as a purebred so he'll be put up for adoption."

"Can we 'dopt him?" Isabel asked.

"That would be up to your *Abuelita*," Darcie replied and cast a scolding look at Archer for putting Pilar in this position.

"Maybe we can take him at the firehouse if she can't." Archer squatted next to Isabel. "I'm afraid I've only arranged to borrow the puppy while we stay here."

"Does he have a name?" Isabel asked, ignoring Archer's comment.

Archer shook his head.

Isabel stared nose-to-nose with the white fur ball.

"Woof," she proclaimed seriously. "I'm going to call you Woof."

"Woof, it is," Archer said, laughing.

Darcie wished she could laugh, too. But once they caught her stalker, Woof would have to go back to the neighbor and Isabel would have grown quite fond of the puppy by then, her little heart breaking at the separation.

And Noah would go back to his life. Darcie imagined saying goodbye and knew without a doubt, she would be brokenhearted, too, but they *would* say goodbye.

"I'm hungry." Isabel's lower lip came out in a pout.

Darcie looked up from the book they were reading and peered outside, surprised to see the sun already setting behind the fence in vivid red splotches. She glanced at the clock to confirm it was around five. "Still an hour or so until dinner. Would you like a snack?"

"Yes, please!" Isabel's mouth spilt in a gap-toothed grin as she flung her arms around Darcie's neck. "Can I have cheese and crackers? That spotted cheese you gave me last night?"

"Cojack?'

"Yes."

"Of course." Darcie planted a kiss on Isabel's cheek and started to rise, but Isabel held firm.

"I love you, Darcie. You are the bestest person, next to my *Abuelita*." She planted a sloppy kiss on Darcie's cheek.

The resistance Darcie had put up for months faded away and her heart soared with joy.

It was time to admit it. She was fully vested in Isabel and her future. She loved the little girl and wanted to have more of Isabel in her life. The joy in loving was worth the pain of loss. She got that now. She may have lost Haley, but she had years of memories. She'd never trade the pain of loss if it meant never having had Haley.

"Can Woof have cheese, too?" Isabel interrupted Darcie's thoughts.

She smiled at Isabel. "He could have cheese, but it's better if we give him a snack especially made for a puppy."

"I'll get one." Isabel hobbled into the small kitchen in the daylight basement and rummaged through the bag of dog items from Archer.

Isabel had the snack in hand and charged past Darcie toward the patio door as she headed for the small basement kitchen.

"One treat only for Woof," Darcie warned.

Isabel frowned.

"He could get an upset tummy if you give him too many treats."

Isabel nodded sagely. "Just like me. I barf when I eat too much candy." She slid open the door, letting in a biting wind.

"Put on your jacket, sweetie," Darcie said, the

simple task of reminding her to wear a coat precious in its own right.

By the time Darcie got to the counter, Isabel was wearing her coat and heading outside. Darcie retrieved the cheese and started humming as she cut long slices. Here was the peace she'd been missing. She felt like she had truly come to the other side of her grief.

She plated the cheese in the shape of a happy face, then circled it with crackers. She mixed a pitcher of juice and laid a place setting by the bar stools before going to get Isabel. Darcie peered through the glass door as Isabel limped around the corner of the house. Darcie couldn't see Woof in the fading light so she suspected Isabel had gone in search of the rambunctious little pup.

Thinking about a way to keep Woof in Isabel's life, Darcie grabbed her coat. Perhaps if Darcie adopted Woof, Isabel could come to visit. That would be a built-in excuse to see Isabel. But were occasional visits enough for Darcie? Not now that Darcie could see how important Isabel had become to her. She'd have to work out something regular with Pilar. After all, Pilar was struggling to care for Isabel and Darcie could help with that.

Humming again, Darcie headed outside. The wind cut through her coat and the dusky night suddenly felt ominous. She'd all but forgotten about her attacker, and that was something she couldn't do. Not yet. Not until Noah came home and told them that the Kerr brothers confessed and her attacker was in custody.

A shiver claimed her body as she rounded the corner to see Isabel step through the upper gate. Woof was nowhere in sight. The gate clanked shut behind Isabel.

Memories of a car running Haley down in front of their home tightened Darcie's heart and fear sent ice water flowing through her veins.

"Isabel, no," Darcie called out and took off running. She scrambled up the incline, her feet slipping on the gravel path. She reached the gate. Her fingers were shaking and she fumbled with the latch.

"C'mon, c'mon, c'mon," she mumbled and finally managed to shove open the gate.

She spotted Isabel on the sidewalk down the street bending down to scoop up Woof. Both were safe, for now, but Darcie knew how a car could careen up the sidewalk in an instant and take a life. Darcie stepped into the yard to retrieve them.

An arm suddenly shot from behind the gate and hauled her into strong arms. She opened her mouth to scream, but a hand clamped over her mouth.

"Scream or fight me and we take the kid, too." She recognized the voice. Her attacker.

She panicked and kept struggling, grabbing at his hand. She found a bandana tied on his wrist. She might not be able to get away but she could drop it as a clue. She clawed it free and tossed it next to the fence.

"I mean it, lady," he growled. "Keep it up and my partner takes the kid, too."

Darcie couldn't risk Isabel's safety. Darcie went slack and her abductor dragged her in the opposite direction of Isabel. Darcie half wanted Isabel to look. To see her being hauled away so she could scream and draw Skyler's or Archer's attention. But then, not only would this creep take Isabel, but merely seeing this happen could also scar the little girl for life. Darcie wouldn't wish that on the precious child.

Please don't let Isabel look this way. Don't let her see me.

Her abductor kept going down the street. Homes sat dark along the way. The occupants were likely still at work and with the light fading fast, even if someone was home, she doubted they could see her. At the end of the block, a car pulled to the curb and the door opened. Another Latino male, wearing Nuevo gang colors, got out. He held a submachine gun. Fear pelted Darcie's heart.

The urge to struggle was strong. She started to raise her arms.

No. Isabel's life depends on your cooperation.

Haley depended on you, too. The thought came unbidden. She hadn't been able to protect her own child from a deadly accident, but she *could* protect Isabel.

With a hand still clamped over her mouth, Darcie pulled in oxygen through her nose, not seeming to get enough to overcome her panic. Her abductor shoved her into the car. His hand came off her mouth and she gulped air.

"Remember the kid," he warned and kept a firm hold on her wrist.

She expected the car would screech from the curb and roar down the road, but the driver eased away and moseyed out of the neighborhood. Likely so he wouldn't draw attention.

Darcie heard Woof barking and Isabel giggling through the driver's open window until the vehicle turned a corner. Isabel hadn't seen her. She was safe.

Darcie sighed out a breath as fear chilled her insides. She was on her own now. All alone. No FRS to help her. No Noah standing tall by her side.

She had to step up her game. Figure out a way to free herself. Her life depended on it.

SEVENTEEN

Noah trailed the Kerr brothers as they departed from the central precinct. They'd admitted to nothing and though he and Judson had questioned the pair for hours, their lawyer had tangled each question until getting answers felt like pulling sticky taffy from a vat. So Noah hightailed out of the building and put himself in a position to follow them in hopes that they'd lead him to the Nuevos.

He kept his focus on the taillights of the oversize black SUV. He doubted they'd suspect a tail, but Noah hung back just in case. He'd checked each of their home addresses, and it was soon clear that they weren't headed to either of their homes, or to the office. It was almost as if they were just driving around with no planned destination.

They suddenly made a right turn and Noah wondered if he'd been made. He took his time taking the corner and spotted them a few car lengths ahead. They continued down the road, so they weren't trying to ditch him. A few turns later, and Noah knew they were driving to northeast Portland. Gang area.

Noah slowed more, even though adrenaline urged him to speed up. They finally pulled into a parking lot at a vacant mall with boarded-up windows.

Noah drove past, found a secluded spot to park and grabbed night-vision binoculars from the trunk. He zoomed in on their vehicle. Michael sat behind the wheel. Randall was in the passenger seat, talking on his phone. Another car rolled into the lot—a smaller, silver SUV. The brothers got out. The driver of the SUV, a short Latino man, did, too. He went directly to the brothers to frisk them. Nuevo muscle, which meant their leader was in the car.

Noah grabbed his phone to call for backup when it vibrated in his hands. Skyler. She was with Darcie.

He pressed Talk. "Skyler?"

"It's Darcie," she said, her tone dire. "She's missing."

"What do you mean she's missing?" he nearly shouted before he remembered his location and controlled his voice.

"We know she wouldn't leave on her own, so best we can tell someone took her."

"How? Why didn't you stop them?" he snapped.

"We didn't see it happen."

"Why in the world not?"

"Because we were respecting Darcie's wishes. Isabel had been irritable and moody all day and Darcie thought it was the stress of the situation getting to her. So Darcie decided to take Isabel and Woof down to the basement for a change of scenery and asked us to stay upstairs."

When Noah had called in earlier to check on Darcie, Skyler had told him about the puppy.

"And what happened?" he asked, barely able to breathe.

"Isabel told us Woof got out of the fence in front yard. She went after him. She didn't see Darcie follow her, but after that, she couldn't find Darcie. We found a Nuevo blue bandana outside the gate, so we think Darcie trailed Isabel into the yard and was abducted."

Their conclusion made sense. At least most of it. "How could anyone find the safe house?"

"Isabel again, I'm afraid." Skyler sighed. "Turns out Pilar brought Darcie's iPad, and Isabel played an online game on it. We think the creep used the phone company to track her signal back here."

"But I told Pilar no computers."

"She didn't realize that included a tablet."

Noah slammed a fist to his leg. "I should have been more specific with her."

Movement ahead caught Noah's attention. He saw another Latino get out of the vehicle and approach the Kerrs.

Noah needed to get off the phone and put his full focus on the meeting going down in front of him. But to do so, he'd have to forget about Darcie. Sure, there was the hope that tailing these guys led him to her location. But that was only a hope. The people who abducted her could have taken her to another location to kill her. Or worse yet… No, he couldn't think about the worst thing that could have happened. Not and go on living himself.

Fear nearly pulled Darcie into the pit of despair, but she'd managed to keep her head and gather as much information as she could from her abductors' conversation. Her attacker's name was Gonzalo. His accomplice was Felipe.

Now there were two of them. Both with big weapons.

They acted like this was a walk in the park. Calm. Joking. They spoke in Spanish, gesturing at her often and laughing as they drove toward the outskirts of Portland. She didn't waste time wondering what they found so funny. It really didn't matter.

What did matter was what they were planning to do with her. She was surprised after all the times they'd tried to kill her that they didn't just shoot her and dump her body. Instead, once they were out of sight of the safe house, they'd bound her wrists and ankles and covered her mouth with duct tape.

She'd tried to ask them what was going on. Why they'd taken her. Why they wanted to kill her. But with the tape it all came out mumbled and only made them laugh.

Gonzalo's phone rang.

"Chico," he said to his buddy and punched his speaker icon.

"¡Hola!" he answered.

"I have told you to speak English," the heavily accented voice said. "You need the practice, or you'll be nothing more than an enforcer for the rest of your life."

"Sorry, *jefe*," Gonzalo said.

"Boss. Say boss," Chico snapped out. "Do you have her?"

"S—yes. We have her."

"Good. Good. Bring her to me."

"But *je*—boss. The others will soon discover she is gone and will be coming for us. We can't risk—"

"It is my decision what we can risk. Bring her to me. Now!"

Gonzalo ended the call and a string of angry-sounding Spanish words raced from his mouth. Felipe tried to pacify him. She took some pleasure in his unease, but she didn't waste time dwelling on it.

Gonzalo was delivering her into the hands of the boss, and that couldn't be good. Couldn't be good at all. She had to focus on finding a way to escape before they reached their destination.

Noah had followed the men who'd met with the Kerrs until he could get Judson to take over tailing them. Now he pulled into the safe-house driveway where a large Klieg light illuminated the forensics staff scouring the area. They were looking for clues to help find Darcie. Large. Small. Anything to lead them to her.

Rage simmered in Noah's gut. He'd failed her. Big-time. And he would be the one to find her. He shot through workers to the porch, where Archer stood, a scowl on his face.

"Man, I'm sorry." The pain in Archer's eyes reinforced his frustration.

"No time for apologies," Noah said, trying to keep a hold on his own emotions. "Just give me the facts."

Archer gestured at the yard. "As you can see forensics is working the scene. Jake's reviewing traffic cams back at county, hoping to pick up the car that her abductor used. And in the investigation, the only item still outstanding is LK Design's financial files. Skyler picked them up and she's reviewing them."

"Okay, so we've basically got squat."

"Basically."

"I'm going to talk to Skyler. Let me know if they find anything out here." His heart heavy, Noah stepped through the door and found Pilar sitting on the sofa, her hands folded in prayer.

"Detective Noah," she said, coming to her feet. "I am so sorry I have caused this to happen."

He squeezed her hand. "If anyone's to blame it's me. I should have made sure you knew not to bring the iPad."

"We can't waste time placing blame," Skyler said from behind her computer at the dining table.

He crossed over to her. "Anything?"

"Files were encrypted," she replied without looking up. "And it took me all this time to break the encryption, but I'm deep in the records now." She pointed at the screen. "Look. Do you see that name?"

Noah stared at the screen. "Rocket Cycles. Someone else connected to the Nuevos."

Skyler clicked through a few more pages and

sat back. "LK Design is laundering money by using money mules."

Noah didn't need Skyler to explain that a money mule was an unsuspecting person who moved money through their own bank account and back to the criminal to make the money appear legitimate.

"I know this name, LK Design," Pilar said from the other room. "It is my employer."

They both spun to look at Pilar.

"What do you do for them?" Noah's words rushed out with the intensity of a discharged bullet.

Isabel recoiled, her eyes widening in fear.

"I'm sorry, Pilar," Noah said. "I didn't mean to yell. I'm not angry with you. Just tell us about your job."

"I book graphic-design jobs for freelance designers."

"How?" Noah asked, making sure he didn't sound so demanding this time.

"My supervisor emails me listings from companies who want advertising campaigns, but he is too busy to do the work. He then asks freelance designers to bid on projects and he supervises them for a cut of the contract. I post the jobs on a website for that purpose. After the bids come in, I consult an approved list of designers and assign the job to one of them."

"Any particular order that you use to assign the designers?"

"Yes, a Ramon Flores has top-priority status and he gets first pick always."

"Flores?" Noah shared a look with Skyler.

"Is there something about Ramon that I should know?" Pilar asked.

Noah shook his head. "What do you do next?"

"I receive payment from the company in a bank account set up under my name, and then I transfer the money to another bank account, minus the commission I make for posting it." She smiled. "A simple job, is it not?"

Simple. Hardly. This was definitely a classic money-mule scheme. She was laundering money and she didn't know it. Likely for the Nuevo gang. Noah didn't have the heart to tell her that she was the connection they had all been looking for and the reason Darcie was in so much trouble.

Gonzalo dragged Darcie from the car by the wrists. With her ankles bound together, she couldn't balance and she hit the ground hard. Pain radiated through her shoulder and down her arm, sending tears to her eyes, but she bit down on her lip to keep from crying. She wasn't about to give them the satisfaction of seeing her cry.

"Up," Gonzalo shouted at her, but with the bindings, she couldn't get to her feet.

He mumbled something under his breath that she suspected was a Spanish curse word, then sliced through the tape on her ankles with a foot-long knife. She got to her feet and he placed the knife at her throat.

"Do not try to escape or I will cut you." He slashed a hand across his throat, and his lips cracked in a wicked grin that sent additional fear racing to her heart.

She knew a large knife in the hand of a maniac like Gonzalo could cause terrible pain. She'd treated horrific injuries on the job. If he used that knife on her, she'd be dead in a moment.

He shoved her forward, and she dragged her feet, searching the deserted parking lot for a way out. They'd stopped at a strip mall in front of a Rocket Cycle store. One of Tom's bike shops sat next door as they led her to the slaughter and the ironic twist almost made her give in to hysterical laughter.

Felipe unlocked the door and Gonzalo pushed her inside. Felipe hurried through a maze of motorcycles toward the back of the building. Darcie knew the boss was waiting for her behind the door, and as Felipe opened it, she came to a stop. Her heart pounded hard. Sweat beaded on her forehead, her hands clammy.

Father, no, she prayed. *Don't let this be the last door in life that I walk through.*

EIGHTEEN

Pilar, Archer and Skyler sat at the dining table while Noah paced. Archer and the criminalists hadn't located any lead besides the bandana. All that told them was that the Nuevo gang had Darcie. Jake and the other FRS members were on the way to the safe house and once they arrived, they'd mount a search for Darcie. To do so, they had to figure out how Pilar's role as a money mule was connected to Darcie.

"Seems to me," Archer said, "the hit list suggests that the Nuevos think the people on the list were possible snitches."

Noah stopped moving and let the idea run through his brain. "Makes sense, but how does Darcie fit in the group? She didn't work for LK Design or even know anything about them."

Skyler sat forward. "If they tracked all log-ins to their computer network, when Pilar started using Darcie's iPad, they would've noticed a change in the login IP and investigated it. And we know they can trace it back to Darcie through the phone company."

"But why wait so long to try to kill her?" Pilar asked, then shuddered. "I have used her iPad for weeks now."

"I suspect it's a matter of numbers," Skyler said. "To move the kind of money the gang needed to clean, it would need a large number of mules. Which means many log-ins to their network. It would take time to go through their server logs to track down the unknown IP address."

"Then, as Archer said," Noah added, "once they discovered Darcie's association with the FRS, they'd likely think she was involved in investigating them, and was the source of their problems."

Archer nodded his understanding. "So they started following her to see if they could determine what she was up to. Which is why they found her outside your house, Pilar."

"Yes," Pilar said. "Yes, they could find her at my home every day as she came to help with Isabel so I could work."

"Aha." Skyler pumped her fist, making Pilar jump. "That means the access from the iPad occurred when Darcie was in your house. They had to think the two of you were in cahoots."

"Ca-what?" Pilar asked.

"Working together to snitch on them."

Archer frowned. "Then why wasn't Pilar on the hit list, too?"

Pilar gasped.

"I'm sorry, Pilar," Archer said. "But it's a legitimate question."

"There has to be a logical explanation." Noah walked the floor, running bits and pieces of the investigation along with what he knew about gangs through his filters. He replayed his department training and briefings, plus conversations with Judson.

"Family. The answer is family." He spun to face the others. "That's got to be it. Above all else, gang members prize their fellow gang members, their neighborhood and their family. They would fight to the death to defend them. Family is so important that their code states that you never mess with rival gang members when they are with their family. They extend the courtesy to other families as well."

"But I am not family." Pilar twisted her hands together. "Or a member of their gang."

"Yes," Noah said, stepping closer. "But you are part of their neighborhood. You have the same ethnic background. And then there's Isabel. You care for her 24/7, which is something they would respect. As such, I suspect they would first give you the benefit of the doubt and dig deeper to see if you're involved before acting. Not so with Darcie. She's an outsider and they'd have no qualms about killing her." Noah paused and hated to add this last little bit, but it had to be said. "It's likely they're still investigating you, Pilar, and they could still try to attack you, too."

Gonzalo shoved Darcie into the back room. The walls held shelves filled with motorcycle parts and a small desk with a computer sat in the corner. Her heart raced at the thought of seeing the big boss, but there was no one in the room except the three of them. Felipe scooted past her and pressed on the corner shelf, which slid open, revealing a secret room.

"Wait here while I make sure Chico is ready for us." Felipe disappeared into the dark.

Her pulse kicked up even higher and panic set in. She couldn't let them take her in there. If she did, she'd be done for. Now was the time to act. But how?

She remembered a self-defense class where they taught women to use what you have and what you knew. All she had was Haley's ring on her finger. It wouldn't help her get free, but it could work as a clue if Noah was looking for her. She slid it off and palmed it. Her panic escalated. This was the last real memory of Haley that she kept out on a daily basis. Taking it off felt as if she was placing Haley on the shelf. And maybe she was. At least the emotions that seemed to weigh her down. They were gone. This attempt on her life assured that.

"They're taking too long." Gonzalo peeked into the opening.

Good. While he'd turned his head, she could place the ring on shelf near the secret door access and hopefully Noah would figure out there was a false wall.

Goodbye, my precious child, she thought as she settled the ring on the shelf. *You'll always be with me. Always.*

Now it was time to subdue Gonzalo. She knew medicine. The body. How it worked and reacted. She could use that. When a person was relaxed, which he seemed to be, the midsection was a perfect target to knock the wind out of them, giving her time to run while he recovered.

She moved far enough from Gonzalo to be able to put some force behind her swing. She intertwined her fingers, then spun and aimed a two-handed punch to the space just below his ribs on the centerline of his body. She applied as much force as she could in an upward motion. Like she was trying to push his stomach into his chest.

"Oomph," he said and doubled over.

She bolted toward the front of the shop. Made it to the door. Twisted the dead bolt. Pushed the door open. Felt the fresh air of freedom on her face. Took a step outside. Breathed deep and took off running. Fast. Down the sidewalk.

Yes, she was going to make it.

An object came out of the dark and tripped her.

She hit the ground. Rolled. Her shoulder, already sore, took the brunt of her fall. The pain sent stars twinkling in her vision. She blinked hard. The object became clear. A foot. A man's foot.

"Get up," the guy said as footsteps pounded closer.

Gonzalo arrived, breathing hard. A string of Spanish words that sounded like curses flew from his mouth.

The man who'd tripped her cuffed Gonzalo's ears. "Idiot. Must I do everything?"

"*Perdón*, Chico."

Chico slapped Gonzalo again. "English, man. English." He gestured at Darcie. "Get the traitor up."

Traitor? Did he think she betrayed him somehow? Was that what this was all about?

Gonzalo jerked her to her feet and she came face-to-face with Chico, his face becoming clear in the streetlight. She'd thought Gonzalo was mean-looking, but Chico's pockmarked face, with several long scars and dark tattoos, gave him a truly frightening appearance. His dark eyes, black as the night sky, narrowed into slits.

He didn't speak. He didn't need to say anything. The message was loud and clear on his face. He was going to kill her himself and his expression said he was looking forward to taking her life.

Noah pulled up to the motorcycle shop. He was acting on a hunch. No facts. Nothing concrete. Nothing that gave him any sense of certainty that he'd find Darcie. But he had to do something. As did the rest of the FRS team. So Noah had called Detective Judson. He'd tailed the men who'd met with the Kerr brothers back to their neighborhood, and was watching them, but there was no sign of Darcie. He recommended that Noah and the FRS check out the motorcycle shops. He gave Noah a list of ten locations and the teams split them up and headed out.

Noah had chosen this location because Judson had said they believed it to be a central hub for the gang.

Noah looked up at the three-story building in an older Portland neighborhood. Retail spaces filled the ground floor, with apartments above.

The rent was way too pricy for gang members to live there, so he wouldn't waste time checking out the apartments. He pulled on the shop's front door and found it locked. Light spilled from under a doorway in the back. He pounded on the door and waited.

Time ticked by. Second by precious second.

He pounded again. Harder. Rattled the door. Nothing.

He ran around back.

Pounded on that door.

Finally, a short Latino male opened the door and waved a baseball bat at Noah, but didn't speak.

Noah held up his badge.

The guy cursed and lowered his bat. "Quit hassling us. We done nothing wrong."

Noah knew the gang task force had been putting pressure on these guys and that he should tread lightly, but he didn't care. He'd cross the line to find Darcie if he had to. He'd do whatever it took.

"I'll just take a look around." He shoved the guy out of the way and jogged to the back room. He drew his weapon and cautiously moved through the doorway. The space held an old desk with a computer and grimy wooden shelves filled with motorcycle parts. He crossed the room to a dirty bathroom that was also empty.

The thug stood, his arms crossed, a smug grin on his face. "Don't know what you were expecting to find, but it ain't here."

"Anyone else here with you?" Noah asked, but he already knew what the man would answer.

"You see anyone else?" The smirk grew.

Noah took one more look at the room but saw nothing amiss, so he wasted no more time and ran for the front door. In his car again, he punched into his GPS the address of the next closest shop. Archer was already at that location, but Noah had to do something.

"She has to be there," he said as he squealed onto the road. "She just has to."

No! Don't go! Darcie's mind screamed as she watched the surveillance monitor and saw Noah run out of the building. She wanted to cry out to him. To tell him she was inside, hidden behind a wall. To run toward him. To run into the safety of his arms. But her wrists and ankles were bound to the chair.

Tears welled up, but she blinked them away. He would come back, wouldn't he? See the ring. He just had to.

The monitor switched to the outside camera. She saw the lights on his car come alive and he peeled out of the parking lot.

"He was so close, was he not?" Chico shoved

her into a steel chair. His deep laugh made her stomach revolt. He ripped the tape from her mouth.

"Noah," she screamed though he'd already driven away.

Chico punched her upside the head. Stars danced before her eyes.

"Scream again and the next punch will do serious damage."

She still wanted to scream, but with Noah gone there was no point, and as Chico had said, he'd hurt her even more.

She turned her attention to him. "What's this all about? Why do you think I'm a traitor? I don't even know who you people are."

"I expected you to deny it."

"Deny what?"

"You have snitched on our leaders and now you must die."

"Snitched about what? As I said, I don't know you or your leaders and I certainly haven't snitched on any of you."

Words rushed from his mouth as he told her some far-fetched tale of money laundering that she and Pilar were supposedly part of and had reported to the police.

Darcie scoffed. "Pilar wouldn't be involved in money laundering. She's far too honorable for that. And I have no idea what you're talking about."

"When Pilar started, she did not know she was laundering our money."

"How does she do it then?"

He explained a computer scheme that sounded very clever. "We have many mules like Pilar and we track them all very carefully. Your log-in to our network with your iPad was a big red flag."

"You've got it all wrong. Her computer broke and she borrowed my iPad so she could keep working. I had no idea about her job."

"Liar," he growled as he bent low, his face only inches from hers. "Our leaders are being hunted down by the police because you infiltrated our network. You will find the same fate as Leland and Ramon. Except I will personally deliver your punishment."

Fear traveled over her body. "What? No! Please. You've got that wrong, too. I don't even know those men."

He grinned. Sick. Twisted. "Didn't say you did. When we investigated you, we also discovered they'd been skimming money for some time. No one takes money from us. No one. And no one snitches on us, either." He jerked her to her feet. "And now it's time for you to join them."

NINETEEN

Noah met Archer in the parking lot and Archer's face said it all. Darcie wasn't there. The other team members had phoned in the same report.

"Now what?" Archer asked, his voice filled with worry. "Where else can we look?"

Noah replayed everything that had occurred that night. He retraced their steps. Something about the first shop kept pricking at his mind. He ran the conversation with the gang member. Over and over again. Word by word.

Dawning exploded in his brain.

"He said us and we." Noah grabbed Archer's arm. "Not I, but we."

"Who?"

"The guy I rousted out at the first shop. He said, 'we done nothing wrong' and 'quit hassling us.' If he was alone he would have said I and me."

"Maybe," Archer said, less than enthusiastically. "He was likely just talking about what's been going on these last few days."

"Maybe."

"Did you see anyone with him?"

"No, but—"

"But you want to go back there and check."

"Yeah."

"Then I'm coming with you."

Noah nodded and they raced for his car. He ran his lights and they made it to the building in fifteen minutes flat. At the door, Noah noticed someone had turned off the light in the back. "There was a light on in the back before."

"Maybe the guy's gone home."

"Let's circle around back and see what we find in the alley." Noah didn't wait for Archer to agree, but jogged around the building, the area familiar from his last stop.

"Back door's cracked open," Noah said.

He didn't need to say anything more. They both drew their weapons and switched from verbal communication to gestures. Noah led the way to the door. Pressed it open. Saw nothing. He signaled for Archer to cover him and he stepped in. He flipped on the light. Nothing had changed since his visit forty-five minutes ago, but using his flashlight, he took a closer look at the desk and shelves. Something glittered in the back. He reached for the object.

Haley's ring. The one Darcie would never remove.

Had the creeps taken it as a souvenir? Was she dead?

His heart refused to beat. He showed the ring to Archer. His jaw firmed, but he then mouthed *clue*.

Yes, right. She could've left it as a clue. Noah directed his attention to the shelf. Knocked along the wood. Hollow. His heart jumped, and he kept searching until he found a spot that gave way. The shelf swung out and they both had to jump to get out of the way.

Noah shoved the ring into his pocket, lifted his weapon, then stepped into a dark hallway. A light was visible in the distance. He followed it into what had to be the suite next door. He remembered the vacant sign out front.

He kept moving. Foot after foot. Step after step. Listening. Hoping to hear anything. But silence greeted him save for Archer's muted footsteps.

Noah finally reached a clearing and found a large room that looked like a studio apartment, minus the bed. Cans of beer sat on the table and ashtrays were filled with cigarette and marijuana butts. The place looked like a party had just ended.

He touched a can. "Still cold."

He went to a door that led into the alley and opened it. He heard movements to his right. Gestured for Archer to follow him. They eased down the alley to a stairway, where he heard voices. They crept up the stairs. The voices grew louder. Finally, he recognized Darcie's cry of distress.

She's alive. Thank You, God.

His heart soared, but immediately plummeted when he realized they had to free her before these killers ended her life.

Darcie reached out and grasped for anything, like Chico's shirt or his arm, but she came up holding air as she dangled over the rooftop ledge. He'd decided he needed to hear her admit her role in the gang's demise so he'd dragged her up there. He claimed that a few minutes hanging over the edge three stories up from the pavement should get her to confess.

But she couldn't confess, as she'd done nothing wrong. She had to pretend so he would put her down, and she could try to escape again.

"Please," she begged. "Let me up and I'll tell you everything."

"Everything?"

"Yes, everything I know."

He eyed her for a long moment.

"I promise," she added.

He jerked her feet back onto the roof, but her legs were made of rubber, and she couldn't stand. She crumpled to the deck and gulped in air to still her racing heart.

"Speak," he commanded.

"I need water." She panted and pretended her throat was too parched to talk.

"Get her a bottle of water," he yelled at Gonzalo, who'd accompanied them up to the roof. Felipe had gone to take care of business, which made better odds for her. Now if Gonzalo left, it would be her against Chico. Even better odds.

Gonzalo trudged to the other side of the roof and disappeared in the stairwell.

She had to disable Chico, but how? Her mind raced over possibilities. Dismissed them as ludicrous just as fast. Time ticked by. She had to hurry before Gonzalo came back.

"What's taking that fool so long?" Chico turned to look at the stairwell.

She had to act fast. She came to her feet. Rubbery legs seemed like they'd collapse, but a burst of adrenaline kicked in. She lunged at him, hitting him below his midsection and knocking him to the deck. She bolted for the stairway.

"Hurry, hurry, hurry," she told herself and prayed she didn't meet Gonzalo on the way down.

"Stop or I'll shoot." Chico's voice came from behind as she heard him race across the deck.

She was almost there. Just a few more feet. She couldn't stop. Not when he was going to kill her anyway.

She heard him chamber a bullet in the weapon. She turned, saw him lift it into position. Suddenly strong arms came around her legs and jerked down into the stairwell. A bullet flew overhead and lodged in the wall.

She smelled his scent, the wonderful musky aftershave and fragrance belonging only to Noah, before she confirmed he was the one who'd taken her down. She flung her arms around his neck and pulled him closer. Her heartbeat refused to return to normal, but she knew she was safe.

Another shot zinged over the wall. She sensed another person moving and heard the other person fire at Chico.

"He's down," Archer said and Darcie's heart swelled with gratitude over his help. He stood and looked down on them. "Since you two are so busy, I'll check on him and call for backup."

Darcie looked up at her friend and smiled. "Thank you, Archer."

He nodded and climbed over them. That's when she heard a mumbled noise below and saw Gonzalo gagged and cuffed. Served him right to endure the same fate she'd suffered.

"Thank You, God, for keeping her safe," Noah murmured. He pushed her back, his gaze feasting on her face. A crease of worry remained on his forehead. "Don't ever scare me like that again."

She smoothed the wrinkle with her finger. "I'll try my best never to be abducted."

He shook his head and squeezed his eyes closed for a moment. "I thought I'd lost you. And there is so much I want to tell you. To do with you. To be with you. I love you, Darcie."

"Me, too. I love you, too," she managed to get out before his lips crashed down on hers. Warm, soft, they crushed hers. The purest joy flooded her heart. A joy she'd never thought she'd experience again. But God saw fit to bring the two of them together.

She thought to tell Noah about how she'd managed to say goodbye to Haley and officially move on, but decided the feel of his lips was too good to pass up. There'd be plenty of time to talk later.

* * *

Hours later, Darcie held Noah's free hand and reveled in her newfound joy as he drove her to the firehouse. They didn't speak. Didn't need to speak, just enjoyed the peace and freedom that arresting her attacker had brought.

He pulled up next to Skyler's car and gestured at the other vehicles in the lot. "Looks like the whole team is here."

"They'll want to rehash everything and it's been so wonderful riding over here with nothing to worry about." She squeezed his hand and smiled. "Maybe we shouldn't go in."

"Ha, like I'm going to take their guff if I don't bring you inside so they can all personally see that you're okay."

"You're the one who found me, so I think they'll be appreciative of that and cut you a little slack."

"Still, a little slack from these guys might not be enough to keep me safe." He went to put his keys in his pocket and stopped to dig inside. "I almost forgot. I have Haley's ring. I thought you'd like to have it back." He held it out in his palm.

She stared at the ring for a moment and knew she didn't want to go back to the cage of her emotions, where she was only half-alive. But she'd love to put the ring in her jewelry box and occasionally take it out to look at it. She took it from him and put it in her pocket.

His mouth dropped open. "You're not going to wear it?"

She shook her head. "This may not make sense to you, but when I took it off, it felt like I was saving my life in more ways than one. I left it as a clue for you, but I also think God was trying to tell me it's time for a change. To move beyond my loss and embrace the living."

Noah circled his hand around the back of her neck. "I hope I count as one of the living that you want to embrace."

"Definitely." She reached up and stroked his cheek, then kissed him for long, joyous moments.

He suddenly pulled back and frowned. "About Evan. I…" He shrugged. "Does it bother you that I gave him up? And the way I did it… Man. That has to make you think twice about me."

She shook her head. "You were young. You weren't ready to be a parent and adoption was better for Evan. Look at Isabel, for example. Mayte wasn't ready for a child—still isn't ready, in a lot of ways—and Isabel has suffered as a result."

"Isabel, right." He slapped his forehead. "I

should have seen that. How did I miss it when it was right in front of me?"

She slid her fingers into his hair and drew him closer. "Sometimes the things right in front of you are the hardest ones to see."

Frowning, he sat back and she wondered what she'd said or done to elicit another frown. "What is it?"

"Evan. I can't simply choose to move on. I think he needs me and I want to get to know him."

"We'll figure it out." She took his hand again. "Together. I'll be by your side and help you find a way to become part of his life."

"You'd do that for me?"

"Of course I will. I'd give anything to have another moment with Haley so I can fully understand your desire to have Evan in your life. We'll just keep trying until we find a way."

"We. I like the sound of that." He smiled softly and she finally gave in, pressing her finger into the dimple she'd resisted since forever.

The firehouse front door opened and the entire FRS team and their significant others stepped outside, all of them carrying work gloves and equipment to clean up from the shooting. Archer was the only one missing as he was still wrapping things up at the crime scene. Darcie suspected that despite it being dark, Jake had wanted to improve morale by cleaning up the house that night instead of waiting until morning.

When they spotted the car, they stood and stared.

"Guess they're trying to tell us something," Darcie said.

"C'mon. The sooner we let them see you're okay, the sooner we can get back to being alone." Noah winked, then stepped outside.

She followed, her body aching from the Nuevos' rough treatment. She walked up to the bright red doors where the team stood. She ran her fingers over the ragged scars from the Nuevos' violence, then looked at her teammates. "I'm so sorry this happened to our beautiful home."

"No worries," Jake said. "Gives us something to do."

"Yeah, like we're not busy enough," Cash mumbled, but his fiancée, Krista, socked him in the arm. They'd been engaged for nine months now and were still very much the picture of happiness, but that didn't mean Krista didn't call Cash on his grumpy attitude.

"What?" he asked.

"Don't make Darcie feel worse than she already does."

"Sorry. It really is okay. As long as you're alive and well."

Noah grinned and circled his arm around her waist. "She's very alive and very well."

"And from the looks of things, very in love," Skyler said.

Darcie blushed and Noah grinned. "I never kiss and tell."

"It's about time the two of you got together." Brady took Morgan's hand to wiggle her engagement ring that Brady had put in place two weeks ago on Valentine's Day. "I thought I was a big holdout on finding the right woman for me, but you two? Man, you guys have been avoiding what was right in front of you for so long maybe you should call the Guinness Book of Records people."

Skyler laughed and stepped closer to Darcie. "I'm so happy for the two of you. I'm also glad everything worked out. FYI, you should know that the DA chose not to prosecute the Kerr brothers. He said it would be hard to prove money laundering. Still, I think Judson scared them straight."

"Let's hope so for Winnie's sake," Darcie replied, thinking that everything had worked out for good.

"You should also know, Pilar was worried sick about you and she feels responsible for putting you in this situation."

"It's not her fault."

"She and Isabel are inside if you want to go tell her that."

"I do." She looked up at Noah. "Do you want to join me?"

"Are you kidding? Of course I'm coming with you." He took her hand. "I'm not letting you out of my sight for a very long time."

Her teammates groaned in unison, but they also patted Noah on the back, signaling their approval.

She and Noah found Pilar sitting on the sofa in the family room, her eyes closed. Darcie hated to wake her, but when they entered, her eyes fluttered open on their own. Trouble lingered in the depths.

Fearing it had to do with Isabel, Darcie hurried over to her. "What's wrong?"

Pilar snatched Darcie into a hug. She smelled like fried tortillas and spicy sauce. "I am so sorry for getting you into this mess."

"I won't have you blaming yourself for something that was completely out of your control." Darcie sat back. "Please promise me you'll stop."

"I will try." She chewed on her lower lip.

"Something else is wrong, isn't it?"

She nodded and tears trailed down her face. "What is it?"

"Isabel. I—I want to take care of her...it's just I am too old to be the mother she needs."

"Mayte will be out of rehab soon."

"I know." Pilar sniffed and took a tissue from her pocket. "But she has finally realized she has a long road ahead of her and even sober, she isn't cut out to be a mother."

Darcie's heart broke for this mother and daughter. Broke for little Isabel. "Who will take Isabel? You have other relatives, right?"

Pilar nodded. "In Mexico, but that is not the life for Isabel. Mayte will put her up for adoption."

"No!" Darcie felt her heart shatter. "No, that's not the solution. There must be someone else."

Pilar's tentative focus locked on Darcie. "I was hoping maybe you'd take her in."

"Me? I'm, I…" Haley's face came to mind and the ring pressed against Darcie's pocket like a burning coal. She wasn't ready for another child…was she?

"It is too much to ask," Pilar said.

"No, it's not. I love Isabel and would be happy to have her in my life. It's just…" She looked to Noah. "We just…we never talked about something like this."

"I'm ready if you are," Noah promised her.

"Wait. Are the two of you, as they say here in America, an item?"

"Yes."

Pilar clapped her hands in glee. "This is such good news. A mother *and* father for Isabel."

"Yes," Darcie said, reaching up to take Noah's hand. "A mother and father for Isabel."

Barking sounded from the game room before doggie footsteps came tripping down the hallway. Woof shot into the room, looked up at Darcie and tried to stop. He planted his big puppy paws on the wood floor and skidded right past her, slamming into a club chair. Dazed, he shook his head and ran back. By the time Darcie picked him up, he was furiously licking her face, and Isabel had stepped into the hallway and was coming toward them.

Isabel. Darcie's soon-to-be daughter. Her heart swelled with so much love she thought it might burst.

Isabel spied Darcie and she started moving faster. "Darcie and Noah, you are home!"

Darcie set Woof on the sofa to free her arms for the beautiful little girl. She swooped her up in a hug. "I love you, Isabel."

"I love you, too." She looked up at Noah. "And you, too."

He circled his arm around the pair of them and Darcie sighed in contentment.

Life was perfect.

Woof hopped down from the sofa and lifted his leg against the coffee table.

"No-oo-o," Darcie and Isabel said together.

He looked up, confused, and proceeded to wet the table leg.

Darcie sat back. Well, maybe her life wouldn't be perfect. She knew that was just for fairy tales anyway, but life would be grand with the three of them and Pilar quite able to fulfill her grandmother roll.

The promise of a happy future with a ready-made family warmed Darcie to the core, something she could never have imagined just a few short days ago.

Thank You, Father.

* * * * *

Dear Reader,

As I wrote the fourth book in the First Responders Series, I really had to work on keeping God's peace in my life. During this time, we moved, I had some additional health issues and we were in the middle of a big kitchen renovation. Opportunities to be frustrated, cranky and without joy were plentiful, and I wouldn't be telling the truth if I didn't admit to letting it all swamp me.

At times, I felt just like Darcie and Noah, drowning and barely keeping my head above water. But then, I'd sit down to write and my own words would convict me. They'd remind me that none of these things are important. That I could let them go and find peace. Which is just what I did. I hope that Darcie and Noah's struggle as they work through tough times in their lives helps with any ongoing struggle you may have to keep peace in your life, too.

If you'd like to learn more about this series, stop by my website at *www.susansleeman.com*. I also love hearing from readers so please contact me via email, susan@susansleeman.com, on my Facebook page, www.facebook.com/

SusanSleemanBooks, or write to me c/o Love Inspired, HarperCollins 24th floor, 195 Broadway, New York, NY 10007.

Susan Sleeman

LARGER-PRINT BOOKS!

GET 2 FREE
LARGER-PRINT NOVELS
PLUS 2 FREE
MYSTERY GIFTS

Love Inspired®

Larger-print novels are now available...

YES! Please send me 2 FREE LARGER-PRINT Love Inspired® novels and my 2 FREE mystery gifts (gifts are worth about $10). After receiving them, if I don't wish to receive any more books, I can return the shipping statement marked "cancel." If I don't cancel, I will receive 6 brand-new novels every month and be billed just $5.49 per book in the U.S. or $5.99 per book in Canada. That's a savings of at least 19% off the cover price. It's quite a bargain! Shipping and handling is just 50¢ per book in the U.S. and 75¢ per book in Canada.* I understand that accepting the 2 free books and gifts places me under no obligation to buy anything. I can always return a shipment and cancel at any time. Even if I never buy another book, the two free books and gifts are mine to keep forever.

122/322 IDN GH6D

Name	(PLEASE PRINT)	
Address		Apt. #
City	State/Prov.	Zip/Postal Code

Signature (if under 18, a parent or guardian must sign)

Mail to the **Reader Service:**
IN U.S.A.: P.O. Box 1867, Buffalo, NY 14240-1867
IN CANADA: P.O. Box 609, Fort Erie, Ontario L2A 5X3

Are you a current subscriber to Love Inspired® books and want to receive the larger-print edition?
Call 1-800-873-8635 or visit www.ReaderService.com.

* Terms and prices subject to change without notice. Prices do not include applicable taxes. Sales tax applicable in N.Y. Canadian residents will be charged applicable taxes. Offer not valid in Quebec. This offer is limited to one order per household. Not valid to current subscribers to Love Inspired Larger-Print books. All orders subject to credit approval. Credit or debit balances in a customer's account(s) may be offset by any other outstanding balance owed by or to the customer. Please allow 4 to 6 weeks for delivery. Offer available while quantities last.

Your Privacy—The Reader Service is committed to protecting your privacy. Our Privacy Policy is available online at www.ReaderService.com or upon request from the Reader Service.

We make a portion of our mailing list available to reputable third parties that offer products we believe may interest you. If you prefer that we not exchange your name with third parties, or if you wish to clarify or modify your communication preferences, please visit us at www.ReaderService.com/consumerchoice or write to us at Reader Service Preference Service, P.O. Box 9062, Buffalo, NY 14240-9062. Include your complete name and address.

LILP15

LARGER-PRINT BOOKS!

GET 2 FREE
LARGER-PRINT NOVELS
PLUS 2 FREE
MYSTERY GIFTS

Love Inspired®

SUSPENSE
RIVETING INSPIRATIONAL ROMANCE

Larger-print novels are now available...

REQUEST YOUR FREE BOOKS!

2 FREE INSPIRATIONAL NOVELS
PLUS 2 *FREE* MYSTERY GIFTS

Love Inspired HISTORICAL

YES! Please send me 2 FREE Love Inspired® Historical novels and my 2 FREE mystery gifts (gifts are worth about $10). After receiving them, if I don't wish to receive any more books, I can return the shipping statement marked "cancel." If I don't cancel, I will receive 4 brand-new novels every month and be billed just $4.99 per book in the U.S. or $5.49 per book in Canada. That's a saving of at least 17% off the cover price. It's quite a bargain! Shipping and handling is just 50¢ per book in the U.S. and 75¢ per book in Canada.* I understand that accepting the 2 free books and gifts places me under no obligation to buy anything. I can always return a shipment and cancel at any time. Even if I never buy another book, the two free books and gifts are mine to keep forever.

102/302 IDN GH6Z

Name	(PLEASE PRINT)	
Address		Apt. #
City	State/Prov.	Zip/Postal Code

Signature (if under 18, a parent or guardian must sign)

Mail to the **Reader Service**:
IN U.S.A.: P.O. Box 1867, Buffalo, NY 14240-1867
IN CANADA: P.O. Box 609, Fort Erie, Ontario L2A 5X3

Want to try two free books from another series?
Call 1-800-873-8635 or visit www.ReaderService.com.

* Terms and prices subject to change without notice. Prices do not include applicable taxes. Sales tax applicable in N.Y. Canadian residents will be charged applicable taxes. Offer not valid in Quebec. This offer is limited to one order per household. Not valid for current subscribers to Love Inspired Historical books. All orders subject to credit approval. Credit or debit balances in a customer's account(s) may be offset by any other outstanding balance owed by or to the customer. Please allow 4 to 6 weeks for delivery. Offer available while quantities last.

Your Privacy—The Reader Service is committed to protecting your privacy. Our Privacy Policy is available online at www.ReaderService.com or upon request from the Reader Service.

We make a portion of our mailing list available to reputable third parties that offer products we believe may interest you. If you prefer that we not exchange your name with third parties, or if you wish to clarify or modify your communication preferences, please visit us at www.ReaderService.com/consumerschoice or write to us at Reader Service Preference Service, P.O. Box 9062, Buffalo, NY 14240-9062. Include your complete name and address.